To dad fu

love

About the Author

Heather Beck was born in Wyoming in 1965 and studied Literature at Columbia University, New York. She emigrated to the UK in 1987 and took an MA in Creative Writing at the University of Manchester and a Ph.D at Salford University. She currently teaches at the Manchester Metropolitan University Writing School where she has developed an online MA in Creative Writing. This is her first novel.

First published in Great Britain in 2003 by
Comma Press
www.commapress.co.uk
Distributed by Carcanet Press
www.carcanet.co.uk

A CIP catalogue record of this book is available from the British Library

ISBN 1 85754 730 6
The publisher gratefully acknowledges assistance from the Arts Council of
England North West, and the Regional Arts Lottery Programme.

Set in Monotype Baskerville by XL Publishing Services, Tiverton
Printed and bound in England by SRP Ltd, Exeter

Home is Where

Heather Beck

One

Over the rims of her husband's bifocals, she stared at the magnetic maple leaf on the refrigerator door: I'll never forget Polly's Siamese twin goose; it was a goose on one side, and a gander on the other.

Mrs Coop pressed two fingers against her lips; then she peered at the map beneath the magnet: there's Polly's directions to remind me. I never had a best friend since Polly. Swallowing, she suppressed the wind welling up in her throat: only thing is I can't make heads or tails of her writing.

She touched the map: well, it's gone smeary.

Whispering, she looked at the maple leaf: we always said we would, but we never did get there to Canada. She bit her lower lip: Malcolm, promised, but he had no intentions of flying. Mrs Coop swallowed again, then tapped her forehead.

'Well, it's all water under the bridge. That's what Aunt Aggie would say.'

She would say it twice. Aunt Aggie always had that habit of repeating herself, even when she belched.

Mrs Coop's stomach rumbled as she felt for the cassette player in the pouch fastened around her waist. With her thumb, she depressed the stop button: I can't hear myself think with all that talk about going home! Blinking twice, she removed her headphones, leaving them to hang around the base of her neck. Then she shuffled from the kitchen into the hallway.

When she reached the door to the back room, she stopped to grin: Fee's scratches always make me smile. Malcolm was furious when she did that; he was fit to be tied.

'That bloody cat of yours has ruined the paint again! Where is it? I'll kill her!' he said.

With the tips of her fingers, Mrs Coop felt the scratches on the door: of course, he re-painted at first, but Fee won out in the end. Mrs Coop tapped the door with the nail of her index finger: after we were first married, Aunt Aggie told Malcolm she didn't want anything changing, and we didn't.

'I was lucky to change my name!' I said.

Mrs Coop scratched the paint: but of course, there wasn't much choice just then: we were still on powdered eggs, never mind avocado coloured paint. She pushed her husband's bifocals back up onto the bridge of her nose. Then she rubbed the skin by her eye patch, breaking a hair that was caught beneath the tape. After that, she reached for the door handle: Fee's catnip mouse, tied by her tail to a string. Fee loved her catnip mouse.

'Just lick her,' I said. 'Don't *bite* her.'

Mrs Coop frowned: that time Fee pulled her tail off, and the catnip leaked straight out the hole in her bottom. Mrs Coop shook her head: I searched everywhere, but I never did find that tail.

She swallowed, then bit her lower lip as she pulled the door towards her. When it was closed, she let go of the handle, then pressed with the heal of her hand against her bladder: just checking. No, I'm not ready yet. She swallowed again. Then she turned and stepped forward to straighten the picture they bought in Blackpool: my vase of seashell flowers.

'Seashell flowers and *grit*,' Malcolm said, and he scratched some blue sky off the corner to show me it's sandpaper they're painted on.

Mrs Coop tapped a seashell petal: well, *glued* then, not painted.

She tilted her head to the left: straight enough. She peered down the front of her cardigan, then fumbled to do up the top button: no seaside weather here. She held her hand in front of her face and blew: it's cold, but I can't see my breath. With flared nostrils, she shook her head at the still life.

'Malcolm, this room's got a pong,' I said.

He told me it wasn't a pong.

'It's the *sea*,' he said.

She frowned: well, he can call it what he likes; the sea never smelled like that with Polly in Southport. I told him I didn't want to go to Blackpool. I told him I definitely *wasn't* going up that tower. I put my foot down at that.

She grinned: I'll never forget that morning when Malcolm stepped on the jellyfish: I did tell him not to take off his shoes, but he took no notice.

'That warning sign by the front door said not to take off your shoes,' I said.

Mrs Coop shook her head: shocking, such language!

She shuffled forward towards the table beneath the staircase, and when she touched it, she jerked back her hand: only thing with these slippers: they collect static. Clutching her fingers, Mrs Coop waited: I must ring *Damart* about my tights. I'll get my chilblains back if they're out of stock much longer. After several moments, she touched the table again with the tip of her index finger: nothing, not a spark.

Breathing heavily, she inched the chair out from beneath the table and sat down too hard on the lumpy cushion: I'll bruise my tail bone doing that one day. I will if I'm not careful. While she waited to catch her breath, she eyed the newspaper and then the telephone. Swallowing, she closed her eyes and pressed lightly against her eye patch while she waited for the stinging to subside: that night I found Fee, she was not here in her chair. Her chair was *empty*.

'Fee,' I called, 'does Finicky Fee want some milk?'

Mrs Coop waited: going into the kitchen, I tripped over her in the dark. I could have stepped right on her, and she'd have scratched me; she'd have hissed then, if she'd have been right.

Only she didn't.

Mrs Coop waited: her coat was soft enough – right thick it was!- but Fee was cold.

She clenched her left hand. Then with her right hand, she covered the end of her nose: I can't see a thing with this eye patch. I told him. I told him I didn't want to go, especially on my birthday.

'Malcolm, I don't *like* your allotment,' I said. 'If you ask me about your allotment, I'll tell you one thing: your allotment makes me *sneeze*.'

'But I've grown them specially for you,' he said, and he wouldn't give over, so I went in the end.

I went to keep the peace.

Mrs Coop's stomach rumbled: I told him I didn't want to go, but he took no notice. He just said my birthday flowers were better than Fee's rose.

'See,' he said, and when he held my hand, I told him not to, but he led me into that greenhouse.

He even had a name for the flowers he'd grown: *Coop's Special Something*. It was something like that. Mrs Coop covered the end of her nose with both hands, then took a deep breath: Malcolm kept talking them up, saying how he'd improved on something he bought from that silly island with a Tescos.

'At least Fee's rose is Lancashire bred. It's not from some silly *island*,' I said.

But Malcolm didn't bite: it was my birthday.

Mrs Coop stared at the carpet: I like that colour, plum. She looked at the door to the back room: it was the day after Fee passed away, and I told Malcolm I didn't want to go to any flower show, but he took no notice.

'Come along; you could do with a day out,' he said.

So I did.

Her stomach rumbled: then we found Fee's rose. I chose one first, but Malcolm read the label and said that the rose would get too big, so he chose one on a small...no: on a dwarf root stock. That's what it said on the label: *dwarf*. She eyed the ceiling, then pinched closed her nose: but after we planted it out front on Fee's grave, that dwarf grew huge.

'*Gi-normous*,' he said.

She frowned: when it first came into bud, Malcolm told me:

'It's *white*! That bloody cat's changed the colour as well!'

'Well, white's not a colour,' I said. (I was always good at art.)

Mrs Coop stared at the door to the back room: of course, Malcolm and Fee never did get on, really. When Fee died, Malcolm said it was unlucky to have a cat die in the house.

'If they get ill, you should *drown* them,' he said.

Fee wasn't ill: she was *poisoned*.

Through arched nostrils, Mrs Coop inhaled: when Popsy died, Aunt Aggie didn't want him laid out in the back room.

'We *eat* in there,' she said, so they put him in the front room instead.

They put him in his uniform.

She inhaled again: of course, Popsy always wanted to be buried in his cardigan, but Aunt Aggie wouldn't have it.

'It doesn't *go*,' she said.

The truth is she hated his cardigan.

Mrs Coop touched the tip of her nose: I chose the tie, though: the red one to set off his face. Aunt Aggie didn't like it. With one thumb, Mrs Coop wiped the corner of her mouth: of course, the red tie *did* set off his face. She dabbed at the patch on her eye: he looked a treat; several people said so. She grimaced, grinned, then swallowed: his Poppet, he used to call me: Popsy and Poppet. I never called him, *Dad*. Swallowing, she pressed her left nose flap, then inhaled lightly through her right nostril: I can't picture it; I can't picture the smell of Fee's rose.

She stared at the scratches on the back room door: fancy taking me to his allotment on my birthday. When we got there, Malcolm was in his element, and the way he was going on about his levelling this and his grades of gravel that, I knew what was coming: a tour of the new path.

She shook her head: by the time we reached that boggy bit he'd fixed up, I told him I'd had enough. Well, I'd already seen it. She wiped the end of her nose: then he walked me back up to his greenhouse, and he was ages opening the padlock.

'Well, what's the point if it's glass?' I said.

He just sang that Max Byegreaves song about the two hands for loving, so I told him:

'Well, they'll just pick up a brick with their two hands if they want to.'

I said so again, but Malcolm only spoke after he slid back the door:

'Just smell *that*,' he said, and he started singing that song again. Then he acted it out with his hands. 'Go on,' he said, and he kissed me.

Then bending, that cane in my eye!

Mrs Coop shook her head: I told the doctor and the nurse I didn't want to go.

'I never liked his allotment,' I said.

Mrs Coop sneezed: they gave him a right good scolding then. He could have blinded me: how would that have been for a birthday present? She pursed her lips: I told him I didn't want to go. She smiled, then closed her good eye: he looked right sheepish in the end.

She waited; then she opened her eye: after I felt Fee, I turned on the kitchen light. She was not her usual shape: her belly was not round, not plump, but *flat*. Lying on her side, Fee looked more like a rug than a cat.

Well, I cried instantly.

Floods.

Mrs Coop inched her hand forward along the tabletop until she touched the telephone. Then she lifted the receiver: there in red, the sticker with the number. She peered over the rims of her husband's bifocals; then she pulled the telephone towards her and pressed the button three times, and when she heard a voice answer, she blurted her emergency.

When she finished, she waited.

'No, it's not me, it's my *husband*!' she said. She stared at the door to the back room. 'I don't *know*!' she interrupted, and she blinked twice.

Then she gave the operator directions, and when she had finished, she closed her good eye, and listening, she pressed gently with two fingers on her eye patch while the operator repeated her directions.

'No,' Mrs Coop corrected, 'out past *Birtwistle* Cemetery, with a *b* as in ball, bounce, and *boy*!'

Nodding, she picked at the tape on the bridge of her nose, then closed her good eye and continued to listen: the stone gate house on the right, past the new estate, the first street on your left just after the four cottages with the black stone and white mortar.

She nodded.

'Ours is on the right, near the end of the terrace. There's a gi-normous dwarf rose out front.'

As she listened, her face reddened.

'It's not blossoming this time of year, not in winter, but it's a standard shape,' she said.

Listening, Mrs Coop opened her good eye, then clenched her buttocks: it's uncomfortable this; there's some sort of lump in the cushion. Shifting her weight to the right, she lifted herself slightly, then felt the cushion.

'What?' she inquired. She prodded the lump in the cushion, then leaned forward and frowned at the numbered buttons on the telephone.

'Not *ten* Knott Steet,' she said, and losing her balance, she sat on her hand. 'It's *seventeen!*' she corrected. With her thumb and ring finger, she squeezed the lump in the cushion. '*Seventeen*, Knott Street!' she repeated.

Mrs Coop jiggled the receiver: maybe a loose wire? She flexed her fingers beneath her: I can't hear a thing with these rings poking into my bum. Her stomach rumbled: I can't hear a thing with all this. She pulled her left hand out from beneath her, then gripped the receiver with both hands.

'Yes, that's right,' she said. She rocked slowly from side to side. 'What?' she asked. She made a clicking noise with her tongue; then she raised an eyebrow. 'No, I said *seventeen!*' She scowled. 'What?…Oh: within ten *minutes*. I see.'

Mrs Coop waited.

'Hello,' she said.

After several moments she moved the receiver to her left ear.

'Hello?' she said. She jiggled the receiver. 'Hello!' she repeated.

She waited, then hung up the receiver: she could have said good-bye first; there's me hanging on for ages. With both hands, Mrs Coop cradled the pouch holding her cassette player, and she stared at the wallpaper beneath the staircase: they're comforting, my pagodas.

Two

Wiping the back of her index finger across both nostrils, Mrs Coop surveyed the area: we planned to have a sink and a toilet beneath the staircase. We'd have a toilet upstairs *and* downstairs then. She wiped her finger on the side of the cushion: it would have been posh then with two toilets. She twisted the cord to her headphones and looked at the ceiling: it was Malcolm's idea after that book I bought him; he even drew up a floor plan: *a bird's eye view*, he called it. He stood beneath the staircase with his bird's eye view.

'You only have enough room to stand up here in this space,' he said. 'That's your highest point.'

Mrs Coop looked at the floor area around her: then he measured it up where you can stand: it was too small. She glanced at the door to the back room: too small, but then he's eleven inches taller than I am.

'Too small? Speak for yourself,' I said.

And he did: there was no changing his mind: it was settled.

Mrs Coop let go of the cord to her headphones. She wiped the corner of her good eye with the knuckle of her index finger; then she looked at the ceiling. After several moments, she felt downwards along the chain around her neck.

'My idea after I misplaced them,' she said, and she put on her husband's bifocals.

Then looking up, she studied the square of ceiling where he could stand to his full height: *it still seems big enough for a sink and a toilet to me.* She gripped the pouch holding her cassette player and stared at the ceiling: *of course, he has to stand back a bit, I suppose.* Unzipping the pouch, Mrs Coop inspected the slope beneath the staircase: *still, he could always go upstairs; there's plenty of head height for him there; it's like standing at the bottom of a well, I always say.* She stared at the slope: *we ran out of wallpaper for that, so he just painted it avocado to match the rest.* She grinned: *he's painted it how many times now?*

'We should have bought more wallpaper,' she said.

Mrs Coop inspected the painted slope down to the point where it disappeared behind the curtain: *at least the curtain blocks off that bit underneath the stairs where it's too low to walk.* She stared at the pleats in the curtain. *We could have had a folding door, but a curtain was easier to fit.* She picked at the tape on the bridge of her nose. *The space below there was no use to me anyway. Let him have it for his tools if that's what he wants.*

'There,' she said as she lifted a corner of the tape. She rolled it back, then rubbed the hairs on her nose while she studied the curtain: *no, just like I said at first: the yellow stripe doesn't go with the pink and the white.* Mrs Coop touched the end of her nose; then she touched the tape: *it's still sticky.* She unrolled the tape, pressing it flat across her nose. Then she stared at the curtain: *besides: I don't* like *yellow.*

She crossed her legs, then twisted her wedding ring: *I don't like* stripes *either. I much prefer pictures to stripes.* She twisted her ring: *a pattern with fruit would have been nice, so near to the kitchen. Something nice in a bowl: apples, maybe.* She flexed her ankle, then looked down: *or plums to match the carpet.* Mrs Coop listened, then flexed her ankle: no. She pressed against her stomach: no, further down. She pressed: there.

'Excuse me!' she said, and she covered her mouth, then looked down at her ankle: it was our honeymoon when I broke it. I wasn't wearing the right shoes for rambling. She rotated her ankle to the right: it's this cold that does it: it's *cracking*! She felt inside her pouch for the cassette player: I'd never been before to the Forest of Bowland.

'Forest?' I said. 'Where are the trees?'

She listened: I hope it's not a robin tapping. When Popsy went, Aunt Aggie said she knew it was coming.

'There was a robin tapping on the window this morning, so I knew straight away. A robin tapping's always a bad sign,' she said.

She was always saying that.

Mrs Coop listened: no: more like that window up in our bedroom. Now there's a strong draught up there on a windy night. Listening, she pressed the play button: it's nice to hear voices. Turning up the volume, she looked at the ceiling: any voice is nice.

After several moments she looked down: not any, but most are nice....some are *better*. She tugged at the hem of her dress: that window always keeps us awake at nights: it rattles. She tugged again: well, it did many a night until we got used to it. At first the rattling got Malcolm going half the time. She shook her head: well, might as well seeing as we're both awake.

Leaning out to the left, Mrs Coop rubbed her good eye, then peered down the hallway: Malcolm never will fix that doorbell, no matter how many times I'm onto him. Suddenly, her good eye widened: no, not the bedroom window; there's someone at the door! She leaned forward and squeezed both knees, then adjusted her cardigan: they say a dog's nose and a woman's knees are always cold. She fingered the hole in her thermal leggings: I wish *Damart* would turn up with my new tights.

'I bet the Queen doesn't wait at least two weeks when they're out of stock,' she said.

She lifted her right foot off the rung of the chair: imagine me *rambling*! She pursed her lips: not a honeymoon as such, more of a weekend away. Listening, she pressed down against the carpet with the ball of her foot: no danger of slipping. It was more of a weekend away than a honeymoon since we both had to work Monday. I scuppered that plan, breaking my ankle.

She lifted her left foot off the rung and tested it against the carpet: I could do with some of Aunt Aggie's knitbone. Shivering, she looked down at both feet: they're *still* draughty, these slippers. I could do with drawstrings, never mind Velcro tabs. Mrs Coop smoothed her hair: it's the unfastening that gets me: you need an iron grip for that! She placed both hands on the edge of the table, and concentrating, she pressed down, lifting herself up out of the chair: at least I broke it *after* Sunday lunch. I certainly took a tumble. First thing Malcolm said was I'd eaten too much roly-poly pudding. She shivered: when he tried to put my shoe back on, I told him:

'No, it's swelling!'

She held her breath: then it started to swell visibly, and he put down my shoe and apologised about the pudding. She coughed: of course, we were out in the middle of nowhere on the top of some hill.

'Now don't go all weepy on me,' he said.

Standing, Mrs Coop stared at the wallpaper in front of her: Malcolm never liked my pagodas. The whole time we were papering, he kept talking them down.

'Well, I just don't see how they fit in with the house: they're *Chinese*.'

Mrs Coop shook her head: well, I couldn't say except that I liked them. I liked them straight away as soon as I saw them. She traced her fingertips over an embossed pagoda: like up close when I first saw Malcolm's eyelashes, and I told him what a waste they were not on a girl. Mrs Coop nodded: what *I* could have done with those eyelashes! I could have been Lower Dunnow's answer to Betty Davis with *those*. She shook her head: when Malcolm took his retirement early, I kept telling him:

'Things'll be right in the end.'

She blinked twice: of course, I never believed it; I had no idea how we'd manage, but *he* did. She nodded, then turned to step into the hallway, and as she moved forward towards the vestibule, she balanced herself against the staircase with one hand: of course, we've had our differences, but we're all right, really, the two of us. She nodded: it was only after Aunt Aggie died that we really came together. We waited a year; then we redecorated the lot: even her bedroom, we repainted.

Standing just outside the vestibule, Mrs Coop stared at the carpet. Smiling faintly, she traced her finger around the edge of the top button on her cardigan: it doesn't match, of course, but it'll do in a pinch. Then gripping the banister, she stared at the carpet on the staircase: I always say it makes a nice swirl that pattern, just like a raspberry ripple, only with plums. She shook her head at the patch of burgundy carpet: naughty kitty, even after Dad made you that scratching post!

When the siren stopped, Mrs Coop turned towards the front door, and squinting, she looked through the glass into the vestibule. Then feeling in her pouch for the cassette player, she listened: we used to have plain glass on the front door, but then he changed it to something special. She pursed her lips:

'What's the point of having glass if you can't see through it?'

Pressing the stop button, Mrs Coop listened: I don't think it's

Damart. She shifted her husband's bifocals to the end of her nose: better, Damart doesn't knock like that. She smoothed her hair, then smiled suddenly: it's him! She straightened her dress and adjusted the sleeves on her cardigan. Peering through the glass into the vestibule, she frowned: definitely no hat though.

She regarded the coat rack inside: Malcolm's hat and overcoat, mine, and the umbrella he found in the bus shelter, the *golfing* umbrella he calls it, big enough for two. She stared at the umbrella: all the colours in a rainbow. She pushed her husband's bifocals back up onto the bridge of her nose: all the colours. How many is that then? She protruded three fingers: Richard of York. When we learned that, Mary Clegg asked Miss Armstrong why it couldn't be Richard of Lancashire. Richard of York did something in something. Mrs. Coop looked up again at the glass in the front door: definitely no hat…his shape though. She tilted her head to the left and reached for the door handle.

'Malcolm,' she asked, 'is that you?'

Mrs Coop listened: Malcolm doesn't knock like that though. She frowned: besides, he comes through the *back* door to save on the carpeting. She shook her head: I swear he makes a point of being late for his meals.

'I'll tell you where I've been: I've been mucking me plot, woman, mucking me plot.'

Mrs Coop swallowed, then let go of the door handle. She took two steps backwards and looked down at the spoiled pattern: there's that stain he made with the oil. It was my fault: I'm the one who asked him to put the chain on the front door after we read about that old dear from Blackburn. Mrs Coop rubbed the patch on her left eye. Then she closed her good eye. She waited, then opened her eye slightly: I bet that chain's hanging down; I always leave it. She blinked: they'll say I had it coming.

'You never put the chain on. Why did I waste a whole Saturday buying the bloody chain and putting it on the front door if you never use it?'

With one hand, Mrs Coop felt inside the pocket of her cardigan: I could do with taking a Rennie's. It's that buttered toast and Marmite getting to me. Withdrawing her hand, she stared into the vestibule: I can see that chain's hanging: it's not across, it's *down*. She swallowed: that old dear from Blackburn: eighty-seven, she was; it said so in *The Chronicle*. Malcolm read it over breakfast: first, they stole her television and her silver; then they stole the rings right off her fingers. Then they…then they…Mrs Coop blinked, then looked into the vestibule: his hat and overcoat are here. Where's he got to then? She looked over her left shoulder at the door to the front room: there's no television. There's no sport on, no cheering. She tilted her head to the right; then she sniffed.

'Malcolm?' she said.

She stared at the carpet, then looked over her shoulder and up the stairs: he probably can't hear that knocking if he's up there; he always goes this time after his tea. She called him again, then waited: it's that fan for the condensation that makes such a noise; I've told him a thousand times.

'Malcolm, if it's the last thing you do, fix that fan!' she said.

Mrs Coop listened.

'Malcolm, get off the toilet! Someone's at the door!' she said.

She looked down at her ankle: that old dear from Blackburn, eighty-seven, she was, a great-grandmother of *nine*, imagine that! In broad daylight! She flexed her foot: my whole leg's tingling. It's that pin in the cold. I'll ask Doctor Khan about that. She frowned: only I never understand a word he says. She stared at the Velcro tab on the top of her left slipper, then shook her head: that time I thought he said, *bill*. There's me explaining how the Health Service is *free* in this country. She turned her ankle to the left: then I realise he said, *pill*, not, *bill*. He wanted to know if I'd taken his *pills*.

Mrs Coop waited: well, *of course*, I had.

She called up the stairs again.

'Malcolm,' she said, 'get off the toilet; someone's at the door! *Malcolm*!' she said. 'Malcolm, is that you?'

Staring through the glass into the vestibule, Mrs Coop watched the front door open, and when she saw the man's bare head, she advised him.

'Malcolm,' she said, 'you'll catch a cold without your hat. You're not so thick on top as you used to be.' Stepping backwards, Mrs Coop felt the wallpaper. 'I don't know: I just *like* them,' she said.

Trembling, she shook her head as the door to the vestibule opened: so after Aunt Aggie died, we painted her bedroom yellow. As the man repeated her name, Mrs Coop stepped backwards until she felt the door handle to the front room press against her spine: not bright, but pale yellow, we painted it.

'Am I right?' you said.

You were right, I had to admit: the buttery colour *was* more cheerful than white.

Unblinking, Mrs Coop watched the man's mouth until suddenly, she grinned: it's not his top lip; it's a moustache: it's *ginger*. Smirking, she dabbed at the corner of her good eye: here's me thinking it's lipstick he's wearing, like Billy Mampy used to on a Saturday. She wiped her mouth: I'd nearly forgotten how he used to wear that make up with his haircut. We all thought it was queer at first the way he dressed like a red Indian on Saturdays. She dabbed at her eye: that wig, it was Mohican, but I suppose we *did* sell more meat that way. Folks really used to queue for ours; not even Duckworth's was a patch on our queue. She pinched the end of her nose: of course, Billy's was one of those with handlebars, and he'd always wax them after his dinner: always tripe and onions or liver, and it used to irritate us the way he chewed. We always told him:

'Billy, it's *dead* already! Close your mouth when you chew!'

She watched the man's mouth move: he's on about something. He's on about something to do with numbers.

'Yes, this is number seventeen,' she said, finally.

She blinked, then wiped her good eye: I shouldn't have said that: he must be a salesman. As her face started to twitch, Mrs Coop felt for her indigestion tablets: he's looked up our name in the phone book like that one did with the double glazing; they're cheeky these days. As she watched the man's moustache, she pursed her lips: no, he's not selling something; he wants an *amount*.

He's repeating it.

Mrs Coop shook her head. Billy Mampy used to chew like Fee did when she caught something. Blinking, Mrs Coop removed her hand from her pocket and stepped away from the door handle to stand in the middle of the hallway: that time in school when the special inspector was visiting, and Mary Clegg reads out her sentence for composition:

'Comfort: on Friday they always *comfort* the rent,' she says.

Well, I'm the one who dared her: but then she said it *twice*.

Mrs Coop stared at the man's mouth: he must be new then. Clenching her teeth together, she put one hand on her hip and pointed; then she opened her mouth:

'It's next door's you want: number *nineteen*.' She flexed her finger, then pointed again to the right. 'It's the one with the white door that needs painting,' she said.

As the man stepped forward out of the vestibule and into the hallway, Mrs Coop noticed the two others behind him. She listened: *my rings?*

'You're not having these!' she said, and teetering from side to side, she hid her hand behind her back.

Then after the man gripped her shoulders, Mrs Coop pursed her lips tightly together, and while he spoke, she shook her head.

'No,' she said, 'no, get out!' As she felt the man's grip tighten on both of her shoulders, she called up the stairs. 'Malcolm,' she said, 'come down *quickly*!'

After the other two rushed up the stairs, Mrs Coop turned her head and glared at the man who was gripping her shoulders. She glared unblinking as he spoke to her, and when he released his grip, she opened her mouth briefly before shutting it as his elbow brushed against her breasts.

Taking care not to touch herself, Mrs Coop listened: *it's those floorboards; they're always creaking in Aunt Aggie's.* She flexed her ankle: *there's a draught.* Concentrating, she stared at the man: *Malcolm always says if anything happens, get a good description; they can track then down nowadays with their computers.*

While her good eye twitched, Mrs Coop looked up and down the length of the man: *nearly as tall as Malcolm. Near enough six foot I'd say. Not fat: skinny. Skinny in a bright green coat with yellow stripes.* She blinked: *they're glowing.*

Holding her breath, Mrs Coop waited while the man unzipped his coat: *white shirt. No: pale blue.* She examined his face as he wiped the condensation from his glasses: *not old, not young either.* As he spoke, she watched his mouth: *he smells of spearmint. He smells of spearmint and cold air.* She flexed her ankle: *I can feel that: it's going. Definitely that pin in my ankle's going.*

As the man spoke, Mrs Coop watched his moustache: *Billy*

Mampy was always chewing on the ends of his. Mrs Coop's nose started to twitch: and when he wasn't chewing, he was always singing. She looked down at her left slipper: only he couldn't sing for *toffee*. Curling her toes, she cringed: well, he came to a bad end, and he deserved it after what he'd done to his own brother. Mrs Coop's good eye watered as she looked up at the man: they were twins. She wiped her eye: not identical.

When the other two men returned from upstairs, the one with the ginger moustache spoke to them, and listening, Mrs Coop flared her nostrils: Freddy Mampy with his own brother's wife….Imagine: how *could* you? She wiped the end of her nose with her thumb: it's the seven year itch she had, but Aunt Aggie had another word for it. Mrs Coop's good eye widened; then she sneezed: Aunt Aggie always called a spade a spade, even to its face.

While she listened to the three men, Mrs Coop felt inside the pocket of her cardigan: they're speaking in code. She watched them as she removed a tissue: they're dressed identical, like those ones were in *The Chronicle*. She wiped her nose: that poor old dear from Blackburn. They'll say I had it coming for not putting the chain on the door. When the man with the ginger moustache spoke to her again, she cupped the tissue in the palm of her hand and pointed towards the front room.

'There's just the television. There's nothing else,' she said.

She dropped the tissue, then hid her left hand behind her back as the two who had been upstairs went into the front room.

While the man with the ginger moustache spoke to her, Mrs Coop stared at the tissue on the carpet. She shook her head as he repeated his question; then she looked up when the two men returned.

'He's in the back room,' she said, and her jaw started to quiver as they disappeared through the door.

After the two men returned, they spoke to the one with the ginger moustache. Then they went through the kitchen and out the back door into the yard, and as the man with the ginger moustache continued to question Mrs Coop, a flush rose from her neck to her cheeks: it's them pulses; I can feel them throbbing in my eyes. I can feel them: they're *collecting*!

'Malcolm!' she said as her earlobes reddened.

While the man with the ginger moustache repeated his question, Mrs Coop stared at his shoes: hoodlums steal them these days. They steal them right off their feet. What do they call them? Not shoes. With her left hand, Mrs Coop pointed:

'*Trainers*!' she said.

Then she hid her left hand behind her back again: someone's great-grandma, just after Christmas. No: just *before*. She bit her lower lip as she stared at the man's trainers; then suddenly, her head bobbed up: it's the front door they've left open; *that's* the draught in my ankle.

Her forehead furrowed as she watched blue lights pulse on the street outside: it's not Christmas; Christmas is over. It's not the lights on number eighteen. After several moments Mrs Coop opened her mouth and pointed:

'It's the police!' she said. 'You can't get away with it; they're here!'

She repeated herself when she saw Mrs Bamber come through the front door; then covering both ears, she teetered from side to side: there's that tingling in my head like when we used to spin ourselves dizzy. She concentrated: if I can just sit down, it'll go. She stepped towards the chair beneath the staircase, and contorting her lips, she blew air from the side of her mouth: that time Mary Clegg and I cracked heads colliding; at first I didn't know what hit me. Then I really did see stars.

'It'll go when I sit,' said Mrs Coop, and she clenched both fists when the man with the ginger moustache grabbed her shoulders.

'Elsie,' said Mrs Bamber, 'I told you to stop ringing the medics. I thought you'd given over doing that.'

Three

Lying alone in the bedroom, Mrs Coop tried again: she stared at the light on the ceiling and began counting backwards until she lost track of the odd numbers.

'One,' she said, finally. She stared at the light; then after several moments, she flinched and looked away. 'It's all spots!' she said as she watched the ceiling. 'Malcolm, I'm seeing them again: it's those spots; they're *moving*!' she said.

She waited.

'Malcolm!' she said, and she elbowed the space in the bed beside her: where's he got to then? She felt across the sheet until she gripped the edge of the mattress: Malcolm always sleeps on the left. He can't sleep on the right, even on holiday. Mrs Coop moved her lips:

'You're like a compass,' she said. 'Only you always point *left*!'

She sniffed: there's no toast burning. He's not downstairs then.

With both eyes shut, she listened: what I could do with is my medication tape. I should write it down what they say: *never shall I rest*. She shook her head: not *medication*.

'My *meditation* tape,' she said, and with her right hand, she gripped the other side of the mattress: well, I'm definitely on *my* side; there's nothing to the right. It's the bed that's smaller.

'Malcolm!' she said, and she let go of the mattress. Then after she finished rubbing her patch, she dabbed at the corner of her other eye: that bruise is throbbing, but it's better than itching. I can stand anything but itching. When I had those chicken pox, Aunt Aggie always told me to leave them.

'Give over scratching, or you'll scar,' she said.

Well, I didn't.

'Malcolm!' repeated Mrs Coop, and without looking, she reached for the edge of the bedside table: maybe I've had him move it? She reached out further: he never puts it back right after I hoover; he makes a point of it. With her good eye watching the light on the ceiling, Mrs Coop stretched for the edge of the table: never shall I *rest* until my good is *best*. That's what Dr. Bellum asks you to say with him at the end of the tape. It sets you right for the whole day, he says.

'I'll try that,' she said. 'Never shall I rest until my good is best.' She frowned. 'No...*good's* not right...It's *better*,' she said, and she fumbled for the bedside table.

***

When Mrs Bamber heard the clatter on the floorboards upstairs, she dropped the card she had been reading, and after a moment's hesitation, she rushed up to the bedroom.

'Elsie,' she said, 'are you all right?'

Seeing that Mrs Coop was still in her bed, Mrs Bamber frowned at the toppled plant stand and the fallen aspidistra. Then she stepped off the carpet in the hallway, and after she adjusted her pinny, she crossed the bare floorboards.

'Elsie, are you all right?' she asked as she righted the stand, then picked up the aspidistra. 'I didn't hear you get up. You didn't did you?' she said.

Blinking twice, Mrs Coop stared at the light on the ceiling.

'Malcolm, it's those spots. They've gone *blue*!' she said. Then she looked towards the creaking to her right. 'Who's that?' she asked.

'It's only me,' said Mrs Bamber. She stroked dust off the plastic leaves as she looked down on Mrs Coop; then she glanced up at the light. 'You didn't switch that light on, did you? I was listening, but I didn't hear you get up.'

'My bed's not right,' said Mrs Coop. 'It's gone smaller!'

'Shh,' said Mrs Bamber, and she put the aspidistra on the windowsill. Then she moved the plant stand into the corner of the room, away from Mrs Coop.

'Well, where's my bedside table?' asked Mrs Coop. 'I want my cassette on my bedside table.' She felt in the air towards her right, then pursed her lips. 'This isn't my bedroom,' she said. 'What's that creaking?'

'It's all right,' whispered Mrs Bamber, 'just go back to sleep.'

'Well, I want to sleep in my own bed,' said Mrs Coop.

'Just go back to sleep,' said Mrs Bamber. 'It's much warmer in here; you can feel the heat from the fire.' She held out both hands. 'See, you can feel it,' she said.

'I can only sleep in my own bed!' said Mrs Coop. 'Malcolm doesn't like it hot in the bedroom. Malcolm!' she called. She curled a lip at Mrs Bamber. 'I want to see *Malcolm*,' she said.

'Elsie, if you don't stop talking, you'll be too tired to see

Malcolm. Now be a dear, won't you?'

Mrs Coop looked away. She stared at the light on the ceiling, then shut her eye.

'Well, where is he? Tell him I want a word,' she said.

'Elsie, just go to sleep,' whispered Mrs Bamber.

Mrs Coop lifted her head off the pillow and looked at Mrs Bamber:

'Why can't I sleep in my own bed?' she asked, and she started to sit up.

'You're all right here by the fire. The medics said to keep you warm,' said Mrs Bamber, and she stepped forward to settle Mrs Coop back into the bed.

'Malcolm doesn't like it hot in the bedroom,' said Mrs Coop. She stared at the ceiling. Then tightening her grip on each edge of the mattress, she counted: nineteen, seventeen, fifteen, nineteen, twenty...*one*! When she heard the floorboards creaking, she swallowed, then turned her head towards Mrs Bamber.

'Is it Aunt Aggie's?' she asked.

'No, it's me, *Dorothy*,' said Mrs Bamber. 'Just try to get back to sleep. You'll feel better for it in the morning,' she said, and she rested a hand on the edge of the pillow.

As her head turned, Mrs Coop stared at the polka dot scarf wrapped around Mrs Bamber's head.

'If Malcolm catches you in our bedroom, sparks'll fly, I'm telling you,' she said.

'It's all right; just go back to sleep,' said Mrs Bamber. 'If you shut your eyes you'll be away in no time,' she added.

Mrs Coop closed her good eye, but when she felt the warm hand press against her forehead, she warned Mrs Bamber again:

'Sparks'll fly. I'm telling you: *they'll fly*!' she said.

'Are you warm enough?' asked Mrs Bamber. 'They said to keep an eye on that.' She hesitated; then with one hand she lifted the blankets.

Feeling the warm air rise against her face, Mrs Coop sniffed: even when I came down with that influenza after Aunt Aggie put me out, Malcolm wouldn't dream of it. He refused point blank to let Polly into our bedroom over night. When she felt a hand on her neck, Mrs Coop held her breath: all Polly wanted was to sit up with me for chance I needed something.

'There's no point in keeping a vigil,' he said. 'She'll be right; just give her time.'

Mrs Coop exhaled, then coughed when she felt Mrs Bamber touch the palm of her hand: it was an epidemic. Polly kept a record after that younger cousin of hers died from it. What was his name? She read it to Malcolm from the list in the paper. 'That makes one hundred and *three*, so don't just tell me she'll be right. What do *you* know?'

Mrs Coop kept both eyes closed as Mrs Bamber tucked the blankets back around her neck: well, however many it was, not one hundred and three, probably.

'Probably less than fifty,' she said. 'Polly always liked to throw in a few more for good measure.'

Mrs Coop's good eye twitched while she sniffed Mrs Bamber's perfume. 'Polly, it's not you, is it? We had a letter from George saying you'd died!'

'It's all right,' said Mrs Bamber. 'It's me, *Dorothy*. You had a bad dream; that's all.'

'Dorothy?' said Mrs Coop. 'Dorothy *who*?'

Mrs Bamber smoothed the blankets.

'Dorothy from next door; who else?' she said. She lowered her voice. 'Now just settle down and get some sleep.'

Mrs Coop sniffed:

'Dorothy?' she said. 'Dorothy Bamber from next door? What do *you* want?'

'Yes, luv, I'm here; everything's all right,' said Mrs Bamber.

'Well, I'm still not signing that petition,' said Mrs Coop. 'Not on Malcolm's account, no way! I'll just do the washing on a Sunday if the bin men want to come on Mondays. I have Sundays off anyway.'

Mrs Coop opened her eye, then shut it as she felt beneath the blankets for the left edge of the mattress.

'Where's Malcolm?' she asked. 'You have it in for him, I know! He never moved that fence, not an inch!'

'It's all right,' said Mrs Bamber. 'I'm here with you; it's all right,' she said as she moved to the end of the bed. 'How are your feet? Are they right?'

'But where's Malcolm?' asked Mrs Coop. 'That stone wall was two feet thick; we *both* gained with the new fence.'

'You just rest for the time being,' said Mrs Bamber. 'We'll visit Malcolm in the morning. It'll soon come.'

Humming, Mrs Bamber stooped to pick up the tartan that had fallen onto the floorboards. She dusted it off; then after doubling it over, she positioned it across the bottom of the bed. 'You must have been kicking in your sleep,' she said.

'But where is he?' asked Mrs Coop. 'I want to see Malcolm *now*.

He's not stopped out again has he?'

Mrs Bamber patted the tartan.

'Just go to sleep,' she said.

Mrs Coop's good eye twitched as she stared unblinking at the light on the ceiling.

'But you won't leave me?' said Mrs Coop. 'You won't leave me, Malcolm?'

'No, of course not. Just get some sleep first,' said Mrs Bamber. 'That's what the medics said,' and creaking the floorboards, she stepped back to the door and switched off the overhead light.

With both eyes shut, Mrs Coop listened; then after several moments she opened her eyes.

'What's that noise?' she asked. 'It's not those falcons nesting on India Mill's tower again? I told Malcolm I can't stand their screeching.'

'No,' said Mrs Bamber, 'it's just the television downstairs. I had it on for a bit of company.'

Mrs Coop stared at the ceiling.

'Is it yellow?' she asked.

'Just get some sleep,' said Mrs Bamber.

'If it's yellow, then it's Aunt Aggie's,' said Mrs Coop.

'Just get some sleep,' said Mrs Bamber.

Mrs Coop closed her eyes and listened.

'I never liked them screeching,' she said. 'I'd sooner listen to a flock of crows!' She opened her eyes. 'I told Malcolm: you'd think such big birds would have more to say than just *screeching*.' Mrs

Coop listened. 'It sounds like they're tearing things….it sounds like they're tearing things limb from limb…it's not *nice*,' she said.

She held her breath; then she spoke again:

'Dorothy?' she asked, 'are you there?…The colour's like butter: it's creamy, the yellow in Aunt Aggie's.'

Mrs Coop waited, then suddenly, she looked to her right:

'Dorothy!' she said.

'Yes, luv, it's all right, I'm here,' said Mrs Bamber. She stood just inside the doorway.

'Dorothy, did you ever hear those falcons?' continued Mrs Coop. 'You know what Malcolm says?' She shook her head. 'Malcolm says they eat pigeons!'

'Just go to sleep,' said Mrs Bamber. Humming, she stepped through the doorway onto the carpet in the hall.

'Pigeons!' said Mrs Coop. 'Did you know we used to keep pigeons?' She lowered her voice. 'Of course, they weren't anything fancy….they were grey mostly, as I remember.'

'That's nice,' said Mrs Bamber. From the front of her pinny, she picked off lint from Mrs Coop's tartan.

'Well, falcons eat pigeons!' said Mrs Coop. 'They snatch them right out of the air when the pigeons are *flying*!' she said as she stared at the figure in the doorway. Then she shook her head. 'Well, that's what Malcolm says anyway.' Mrs Coop waited, listening as she watched Mrs Bamber in the doorway. 'Dorothy?' she said.

'Just go to sleep,' said Mrs Bamber. She dropped the lint onto the carpet, then picked it up and put it in her pocket. She waited a moment, then took another step backwards.

'Dorothy?' said Mrs Coop, 'what's that noise?'

'It's just me humming,' said Mrs Bamber. 'My mother always likes it when I hum,' she said as she poised herself on the edge of the landing.

'Oh, that's nice,' said Mrs Coop. She looked towards the foot of the bed, and concentrating, she flexed her ankle until she felt it crack; then she looked back at the doorway. 'Dorothy, I can't see you,' she said. 'You won't leave me?'

'No, I'm here,' said Mrs Bamber. 'I'm here with you all night,' she said, and she continued to hum.

'That's nice,' said Mrs Coop; then she frowned. 'When those falcons…when those *peregrines* came to nest on the India Mill's tower, Aunt Aggie said it was a bad omen.' Nodding, Mrs Coop watched the gas fire. 'Aunt Aggie was always saying that, but of course, she never liked the India Mill. She said the Lower Star Mill was better: it was smaller but they treated you right, she said.'

'Just go back to sleep, Elsie; you're babbling,' said Mrs Bamber, and she took a deep breath, then started to hum more loudly.

Mrs Coop listened: I don't know that tune. I don't know that tune at all. She opened her mouth, then shut it: no: she'd think I'm daft for asking.

'Dorothy,' she asked, 'did you know my Aunt Aggie?'

She waited, then asked again several times before Mrs Bamber stopped humming.

'No,' said Mrs Bamber, finally.

'Well, did you know my Aunt Aggie was scalped at India Mill?' she said.

'Just try to nod off now; you don't want any more bad dreams,' said Mrs Bamber, and she continued to hum.

Aunt Aggie was in a bad way near the end: well, she was eighty-seven. Malcolm kept saying so:

'They shoot animals in her condition; I don't want her dying in the house,' he'd say.

Well, she didn't.

Mrs Coop grinned: *tantalisers*, Aunt Aggie always called her tranquillisers that. Feeling a draught against her face, she started to speak again:

'After Aunt Aggie's hair got caught up, that was the end of her job. They didn't ask twice what happened.' Mrs Coop puffed out her cheeks, then counted to one and expelled the breath she had been holding. After that, she continued. 'Do you know what they said? They said she should have had her hair tied back. *Those were the rules*, they said, and they were all for fining *her*!'

Mrs Coop listened to Mrs Bamber's humming. Then after several moments she continued:

'But my Aunt Aggie had beautiful hair. It was black like the colour of *treacle*!' she said.

'I'll just turn out this light in the hallway,' said Mrs Bamber. 'That should help you sleep.'

After Mrs Bamber disappeared from view, Mrs Coop continued to watch the doorway, and when the light went out, she blinked.

'Don't leave me,' said Mrs Coop.

'I'm not leaving you,' said Mrs Bamber. 'I'm just popping downstairs; I won't be a minute.'

'But I didn't hear the bell go,' said Mrs Coop. She frowned, then continued to speak in the darkness:

'It was those falcons nesting that did it. Aunt Aggie never caught her hair in anything before those falcons, before those *peregrines*.' From the bed, Mrs Coop watched the gas fire. 'Afterwards, she had to comb her hair forward to cover her spot. That's what she called it.' Mrs Coop freed her hand from beneath the blankets, then rubbed both eyes. 'Well, it was more than a *spot*,' she said.

She watched the fire.

'Dorothy, I'll tell you something I've never told anyone: I was never happier than when that man on Nancy Street shot those falcons.' Mrs Coop raised her voice. 'No more screeching!' she said; then she frowned at the fire. 'Of course, that was *after* Aunt Aggie passed away.' She nodded. 'I suppose it was a different pair of falcons he shot, but they were definitely related: *definitely, they were related!*' she said.

She listened.

'That's not a robin tapping, is it?' she asked.

Staring at the gas fire, she waited. Then she turned her head to look at the ceiling, and after several moments she started to count down out loud, but when she lost track of the numbers she stopped and stared without speaking at the fire: of course, it was cruel in a way to shoot the falcons. She flexed her ankle: it's cold. She listened: never mind Dorothy's '*I won't be a minute*;' Malcolm's got her pegged. He always says so.

'No, she won't be a *minute*; she'll be half an hour, *easy*.'

Yawning, Mrs Coop shut her eyes: when the Council gave Malcolm his gold watch, he used to time her, and then he'd always ask me after:

'How come it only takes you two minutes, but it takes her *ten* just to settle with the milkman?'

Tilting her head to the left, Mrs Coop nodded.

She nodded again.

Then when her mouth opened, she started softly to snore.

Four

After the doorbell sounded again, Mrs Coop shut her eye and clenched her fists: there's that. There's that *st*...It's *stabbing* that pain in my neck.

'St, st, st...Turnips!' she said. She opened her good eye and stared at the curtain in front of her. 'I hate them *stripes*!' she said as she leaned back in the chair. She waited, then unclenched her fists: no, just aching. Aching just there at the base of my neck. I'll need two for it. I'll definitely need two tablets. She puffed her cheeks out at the curtain.

'It's them. It's them *what's its* again. I *hate* them stripes!' she said. Then she sniffed and leaned out towards her left to look down the hallway. 'What's...who's that moving...movement?' she said. 'What?' She winced at the stab of pain, and as she rubbed the patch on her eye, she listened. 'Not more stripes?' she said. Her good eye watered as she tried to focus on the approaching figure: Aunt Aggie used to tell me about that girl at Lower Star Mill with the glass eye. She never tired of telling me that.

'You'd ask her to keep an eye on your frames, and she'd take her eye out and put it on one of your frames while you went to the toilet,' Aunt Aggie always said.

'Oh, there you are!' said Mrs Bamber. 'You gave me a start

sitting there. I thought you'd still be in bed when you didn't answer the door.' She clutched the bottle of milk with both hands. 'I almost dropped this when I saw you,' she said.

Mrs Coop stared at Mrs Bamber's pinny: Aunt Aggie loved to tell that story about the girl with the glass eye. It was only when I heard Freddy Mampy's that I realised it wasn't true. She tilted her head as she noticed the milk bottle: Freddy's story was the same, only it was an old butcher he knew with a glass eye he used to keep on his till. Shivering, Mrs Coop curled her lip at the stripes on Mrs Bamber's pinny.

'I hate them!' she said, and her jaw trembled. 'I *hate* them!' she repeated, and with one hand, she took a swipe at the pinny.

'It's all right, luv,' said Mrs Bamber. 'It's only me: *Dorothy*.' She gripped the milk bottle closer to her chest and watched while Mrs Coop clasped her hands together in her lap; after Mrs Coop had turned her head away to face the curtain beneath the staircase, Mrs Bamber stepped forward. 'Why Elsie,' she said, 'your lips have gone right *blue!*' Frowning, she set the milk on the table, then touched Mrs Coop's face. 'Here,' she said, 'just let me feel you,' and she bent suddenly to unclasp Mrs Coop's fingers. 'Oh, I *am* sorry!' she said, and she bobbed up just as suddenly and wiped her hands on her pinny.

With the tip of her tongue, Mrs Coop inspected the lump on the inside of her cheek; then jawing gently against it, she regarded Mrs Bamber.

'I *hate* them!' she said.

'It's all right, luv,' said Mrs Bamber, 'You must have been dreaming.' She glanced at Mrs Coop's lap, and with the back of one hand, she reached out. 'Your cheeks are cold too,' she said. 'It's a good thing I came by early. The temperature's dropped, you know. There's a frost outside this morning!'

Mrs Coop flared her nostrils:

'What's that smell?' she asked. She licked her lips and made a sour face. 'It's not right, that smell,' she said.

Mrs Bamber lifted the telephone off of the table and placed it back onto the receiver.

'It's a good thing I had the medics sort that phone out; it had me worried all night,' she said, and she wagged a finger at Mrs Coop. 'I told them I thought you might try ringing again, so we decided it was best left unplugged like we did the last time.' Mrs Bamber put her hand on her hip and regarded the patch of saliva on the front of Mrs Coop's frock. 'You've got to stop ringing them,' she said. 'It's been weeks; I thought you'd given over doing that.'

Mrs Coop stared at the ceiling.

'There's plenty of room under here for a toilet. We wouldn't have to go upstairs then,' she said.

Nodding, Mrs Bamber examined herself in the mirror next to the souvenir collage from Blackpool.

'I had to rush this morning,' she said. 'There was barely enough time to get myself sorted before our Petula came around.' She removed the remaining curler from her fringe, then sprang the hair pin open and clamped it onto the front of her pinny. 'I'll just put the fire on for you,' she said as she slipped the curler into a pocket on the front of her pinny. Then she arranged her fringe, spreading the curl evenly across her forehead. After that, she turned away from the mirror and pointed at Mrs Coop's lap. 'You sort yourself out, then go and get a warm,' she said, and she disappeared into the back room.

Mrs Coop licked her lips as she felt the wallpaper pagodas. She sniffed: not lipstick, but something. Something *like* lipstick. She listened: what's that smell for when the gas is leaking? She flexed her toes, then pressed her heel against the carpet: my ankle aches. I should ask about wrapping it. She looked up at the ceiling:

'I think my wrap is upstairs,' she said. 'I think it's upstairs on my table next to my medication tape.'

Carrying a box of tissues, Mrs Bamber returned from the back room.

'I was worried last night,' she said. 'I thought you'd wake up again and not know where you were, so I was listening, but you were very quiet. Here,' she said. She plucked several tissues from the box, then held her hand out towards Mrs Coop. 'I told you to knock on the wall with your cane if you needed anything. Do you remember?' She lowered her voice. 'You'll just want to sort yourself out,' she said.

Mrs Coop continued to examine the wallpaper; then after several moments, she touched the tip of her nose.

'What's that smell?' she asked.

Mrs Bamber sniffed:

'I don't smell anything,' she said.

Mrs Coop insisted:

'There's that smell, like with the gas,' she said. 'What's it called?' She pointed. 'There,' she said. 'It's just there: a *fume*.'

Mrs Bamber sniffed:

'Oh, you mean the fire,' she said. 'That'll go once the room heats up.'

Mrs Coop turned her head to the left, and when she saw Mrs Bamber's pinny, she waited: no, it's not stabbing; it's just aching. My neck's aching: I wonder did I nod off? I don't remember coming down this morning.

'It's the cold. Malcolm, I need my tablets,' she said. Then her good eye widened in recognition. '*Dorothy?*' she asked, and she tapped a finger on the table. 'I was thinking this morning I wanted to ask you something.' She corrected herself. 'No: *tell* you, it was. I remembered I wanted to *tell* you something.'

Mrs Bamber waved the tissues over Mrs Coop's lap.

'Yes, luv: you'll just want to sort yourself out first,' she said. 'There's no use talking until you're right.'

Mrs Coop sniffed, then focused on Mrs Bamber's head: there's no scarf. There's no polka dots, but the pinny's right. It's definitely Dorothy's. It's like my old apron with the blue and white stripes.

'Dorothy,' she said, 'I wanted to tell you what I remembered about something you were asking last night…no: *yesterday.*'

Mrs Bamber dropped the clump of tissues onto Mrs Coop's lap.

'Just sort your teeth out,' she said. 'There's plenty more tissues if you need them.'

Mrs Coop rubbed her eye patch: I don't remember hearing the bell. She flexed her ankle: I don't remember letting Dorothy in.

'When I let you in, was I some time coming? I told Malcolm that bell's not working,' said Mrs Coop.

Mrs Bamber pointed at Mrs Coop's lap.

'The bell's fine. Just sort yourself out, luv,' she said. 'My mother's teeth pop out all the time. You're all right; I'm used to it.'

Mrs Coop wiped the corner of her good eye: I wonder, did I nod off? She looked at Mrs Bamber:

'Was I some time coming? I told Malcolm that bell's not right,' she repeated. 'What?' she said as she noticed Mrs Bamber's finger.

Mrs Bamber flexed her finger again and pointed at Mrs Coop's lap:

'It's your teeth,' she said, and with her other hand, she reached to lift the clump of tissues. 'See: it's your teeth,' she said. 'I'll just put the kettle on while you pop them back in. Then go and get yourself a warm by that fire; you're freezing!' she said, and she dropped the tissues back onto Mrs Coop's lap, then picked up the bottle of milk and stepped into the kitchen.

Kicking a foot against the table leg, Mrs Coop felt for the glasses on the chain around her neck. Then yawning, she lifted the tissues; she put her teeth in, then rubbed her neck. After that, she drummed her fingers on the telephone table and listened to Mrs Bamber humming in the kitchen. When she smelled toast, she turned slightly in her chair: maybe Malcolm was having his buttered toast and Marmite? Maybe that's why I came down? He always burns it when he comes in late smoking those cigars.

'Dorothy, is there Marmite?' she asked.

'No, luv, it's tea. I'm making you a nice cup of tea!' said Mrs Bamber. 'Now go and get by that fire,' she said, and she put two more slices of bread in the toaster.

Concentrating, Mrs Coop placed a hand on the telephone table, then tried to lift herself out of the chair. She paused to remove the clump of tissues from her lap, then tried again: it's no use. I've gone stiff. She inspected her frock: well, I'm dressed, so I can't have been down here all night, at least. She flexed her ankle: at least my ankle's not so stiff, considering. Frowning, she stared at the curtain: I don't remember hearing that bell though. She inspected her wrist: there's no watch. I must have nodded off.

Mrs Coop settled back in the chair and stared at the curtain: what *were* they thinking when they put that yellow stripe in with the pink and the white? Her stomach rumbled: I told Malcolm I would've preferred something with pictures, some fruit or flowers being so close to the kitchen. She sucked in her stomach: I'll never forget that Willacy girl behind the counter with her belly button showing in the middle of winter. I'd never seen anything like it, and there's Malcolm with his bird's eye view. Of course, the Willacy girl couldn't give a peanut, but Malcolm carries on anyway about the space he's drawn out, how it's such and such a width and such and such a height, and on and on he goes until even I'm staring at the Willacy girl's belly button. Then as Malcolm shows her how much he has to stoop below the stairs, the Willacy girl snaps her fingers:

'I know: stripes would make it *look* taller!' she says.

I could have groaned. I told him straight away:

'I *hate* stripes,' I said, but he took no notice.

Then out trots the Willacy girl with her stripey material.

'See how soft it is? That's velvet!' she says, and when she's unrolled the material she looks him in the eye. 'Go on, feel it,' she says.

Mrs Coop's stomach rumbled: the way she's looking at him, I could have been *invisible*.

Then the Willacy girl bends over and strokes out the material until her stripes lie flat along the whole length of the counter, and I could tell straight away what it'd look like: it'd look like a beach chair; it wouldn't look right in the house.

'That *is* soft,' says Malcolm, and he's stroking each colour of stripe. 'I can't tell which colour is softest,' he says. Then he turns to me. 'Just feel this, Elsie. Soft, isn't it, for a pair of curtains?'

Mrs Coop snorted: as if he spends all his time padding about the house stroking the curtains!

As she leaned forward, her ankle cracked. Then after several attempts, she gripped a handful of velvet stripes: I'm always telling him how tight he is; then when the Willacy girl rang everything up, Malcolm didn't even hesitate about the cost. Mrs Coop loosened her grip. She rubbed the velvet between her thumb and forefinger, then let go of the curtain: well, I'd never seen him with a roll of bills like that before. I asked him, but I'd no joy.

'Have you still not got by that fire?' said Mrs Bamber, and she swallowed toast crust while Mrs Coop tried to lift herself out of the chair.

'This chair's too low!' said Mrs Coop.

Mrs Bamber wiped a crumb from the corner of her mouth, then extended a hand:

'At least you tried first,' she said as she helped Mrs Coop out of the chair. 'I always tell Mother: *just try it yourself first*, I say, and she does….well, *generally* she does.'

When she had escorted Mrs Coop to the rocking chair in front of the fire, Mrs Bamber removed the shawl that was folded over the arm of the other chair, and humming, tucked it around Mrs Coop's legs.

'You get yourself warm,' she said as she patted Mrs Coop's knees. 'I won't be a minute,' she added as she left the room.

'No, you never are,' said Mrs Coop, and she inspected her wrist. Then she looked at her slippers: when I wore them to bed that time, Malcolm drew the line. He slept in Aunt Aggie's room instead. Mrs Coop clutched her stomach: well, I don't know what he expects coming in at all hours.

Shivering, she watched the fire: I prefer coals; coals are more interesting, but Malcolm wanted gas after Aunt Aggie died. She grinned: when he first said so, I thought he meant wind. I couldn't understand why he wanted wind.

'Here, this'll warm you up,' said Mrs Bamber, and she held a cup of tea out for Mrs Coop.

Pressing the heal of her hand against her stomach, Mrs Coop

looked at the teacup:

'That's not my mug,' she said.

'Well, that's all right,' said Mrs Bamber. 'It'll taste just the same. Here, try it,' she said.

When Mrs Coop touched the cup, she withdrew her hand and blew on her fingers.

'No, it's too hot. I can only have it from my mug,' she said, and she pressed her feet against the fender.

'Well, you never complained before,' said Mrs Bamber, 'and when I made you a cup yesterday, you said you liked it!'

'No, I didn't,' said Mrs Coop. 'I can only have it from my mug,' she insisted, and she blinked twice.

'Well, I'll just set it here for you,' said Mrs Bamber, 'and you can have it when it cools down if you like. There's toast as well. There's toast and marmalade. Do you want me to do you anything else?'

'No, I've eaten,' said Mrs Coop, and avoiding the hot teacup, she reached for the toast. 'I prefer plain bread with butter. It doesn't grow on trees, you know,' she said.

Mrs Bamber shook her head while she stared at the swelling around Mrs Coop's eye patch. After several moments, she spoke again:

'I've already put your bin out. Is there anything else you want washing while I'm doing your sheets?'

Mrs Coop pressed her feet harder against the fender: I can feel it warming through my soles.

After wiping crumbs off the leatherette, Mrs Bamber sat on the edge of the armchair.

'I rang the hospital this morning, and the nurse on duty, that nice one with the posh accent and the club foot, she agreed with me that Malcolm might wake up any day now,' said Mrs Bamber, and she leaned back, relaxing in the chair. 'So that's good news, isn't it?' she said.

Mrs Coop nibbled at the crust before she set her toast in the ashtray on the table between them. Then she wiped her mouth and looked at her wrist:

'Is my watch back yet? I want to see Malcolm,' she said.

Mrs Bamber leaned forward and moved the ashtray to her side of the table; then she raised her voice. 'We'll go see Malcolm again later this morning. I have to go around to our Petula's first; she needs a lift with her ironing,' she said, and she watched as Mrs Coop clasped both knees and stared at the rug in front of the fire; then after several moments, Mrs Coop's lips moved as she flexed her feet, then rubbed behind each ear.

'What?' said Mrs Bamber. 'I'm sorry; I can't hear what you're saying.' She tested the firmness of the curls around her ears, then continued. 'We'll get him some more flowers. I know they won't be a patch on his own, but he might appreciate the scent,' she said, and she twisted the gold posts on her new earrings.

'It's freesias,' said Mrs Coop.

'Don't worry,' said Mrs Bamber. She glanced at the fire. 'You'll warm up in a moment.'

After rubbing behind both ears, Mrs Coop wiped a dew drop from the end of her nose.

'I was first one in,' she said, and she stared at the rug in front of the fire.

Mrs Bamber sniffed:

'What's that, luv?' she asked.

'I was first one in,' repeated Mrs Coop, and she rubbed behind her ears as Mrs Bamber set her cup of tea on the table. 'I went first in the bath on Fridays, unless Polly was stopping over; then I went second. Of course, Polly had a habit of splashing.' She stared at the gas flames, then eyed Mrs Bamber. 'Polly was my best friend, but she emigrated to Canada,' she said.

'I have three sisters back in Yorkshire,' said Mrs Bamber. She tweaked both her earlobes. 'Except for Mary; she's dead now. She was only forty-one when it happened.' She blushed. 'I'm sorry,' she said. 'Are you sure you won't try that tea now? It should be cool enough.'

'Malcolm always says I run my baths too hot,' said Mrs Coop. She flexed her feet against the fender. 'Of course, Polly didn't mind: she liked her baths piping as well.'

Sniffing, Mrs Coop flared her nostrils: it's clinging, that smell.

'We'll go see Malcolm later this morning after I've been to Petula's,' said Mrs Bamber. 'We'll take him some roses. Now I'll just see about those sheets in your bedroom,' she said.

A flush rose in Mrs Coop's cheeks.

'I can do my own washing on *Sunday*,' she said.

'No, you're all right; I won't be a minute,' said Mrs Bamber. 'We'll go and see Malcolm just as soon as I get back,' she said. 'We'll take him some roses.'

Mrs Coop looked at her wrist.

'But I don't have the time,' she said.

'It's all right. I'll come and get you like I always do,' said Mrs Bamber.

'But I don't want to be late,' said Mrs Coop. 'I don't want to be late if there's only an hour. I need my watch,' she said.

'Don't worry; you won't be late,' said Mrs Bamber. 'I'll come and get you in plenty of time.' She sniffed, then pointed at Mrs Coop's feet. 'I thought I smelled something; it's the rubber on your slippers! You'll have to move them off that fender.'

Pinching the end of her nose, Mrs Coop looked at her feet while Mrs Bamber repositioned them on a cushion just outside of the fender.

'There,' said Mrs Bamber, and she patted the cushion. 'That's just as comfy, isn't it?' She scratched her head, then felt inside the pocket of her pinny. 'Now I'll just have a look upstairs,' she said. She stood, then felt both her earlobes. 'I won't be a minute,' she added as she rotated her earrings.

'My medication tape is up there,' said Mrs Coop, 'and my wrap: my wrap for my ankle is in my bedroom,' she said.

'Yes,' said Mrs Bamber, 'I'll just have a look.'

After Mrs Bamber had gone, Mrs Coop sneezed, then reached for the remains of her toast: of course, I prefer bread and butter. Freddy Mampy always used to say tripe was his bread and butter.

'Tripe's out best seller,' he said.

When Mrs Coop felt the glass ridges on the edge of the ashtray, she frowned:

'I thought that was a plate,' she said. 'I keep telling Malcolm not to, but he always smokes in the house.'

Five

Shading her eyes, Mrs Coop stared out the hospital window: it's dazzling, the sunshine: it's frosty! She surveyed the sky: there's no clouds; that's unusual.

'I won't be a minute. I just want a word with the nurse,' said Mrs Bamber, and she let go of Mrs Coop's coat sleeve.

'It's like that day we saw the Isle of Man from Blackpool Tower,' said Mrs Coop. She looked down at her gloves, then altered the grip on her cane: only it was a summer day then...well, evening, and it was a *warm* sky. 'It wasn't frosty,' she said, and she stared down at the buildings: Dorothy always says she likes the view from up here.

'Look, you can see the whole town!' she says.

Mrs Coop scowled at the buildings: well, who wants to look at all that clutter? Gripping her cane tighter, she watched the sky as the nurse on reception hung up the telephone, then greeted Mrs Bamber:

'Are you all right this morning?' she said.

'I'm not so bad,' said Mrs Bamber. 'At least it's not raining.' She lifted her hair away from her ears. 'See,' she said, 'I've finally gone through with it; you don't think I'm too old to carry it off?' she asked.

While Mrs Bamber discussed her ears with the nurse, Mrs Coop scanned the hilltops: of course, those aerials are an eyesore. I remember when they first went up. There was an outcry. Cupping her hand behind her ear, Mrs Coop watched the aerials; then she looked down: when Dorothy says that about the view, I always tell her the town spoils the scenery. She inspected the view: no, those tower blocks by the football ground are gone now. I keep forgetting. She turned her head to address Mrs Bamber: no, I won't bother; she says I'm just to ignore that drilling on the road.

Listening, Mrs Coop shaded her eyes as once more she looked out the window: there's St. John's spire. I don't believe that story about the gypsies who climbed it to get the gold. It's too steep, and there's still plenty of gold showing on that weathervane. She pressed her bladder: no, I'm all right for the time being. She grinned at the gold: the last time I was in St. Johns was for its re-opening. There must have been hundreds there to see that new window. I'll never forget Aunt Aggie: she thought they should be ashamed about their new window having stains on the glass. Of course, she was well on her way then. Mrs Coop pressed her bladder again: no, there was that baptism I went to with Aunt Aggie; that was the last time, but it was in a chapel that stank of mildew off to the side of the main bit. Aunt Aggie said so through the whole baptism. That's all she said after as well. It was embarrassing eating those sandwiches with everyone listening about the mildew. Wiping her mouth, Mrs Coop regarded St. Johns: of course, I'm not religious, but it was beautiful, that stained glass window: it was *heavenly*.

Raising an eyebrow, she regarded the zeppelin hovering above the football ground: well, what's that then, an aeroplane? Malcolm can't sleep with aeroplanes going over: they make a *rumble*. Gripping her stomach, Mrs Coop started at the sound of the nurse's voice:

'And how's Mrs Coop this morning?' repeated the nurse.

'Oh, she's fine,' answered Mrs Bamber.

'I want to see Malcolm,' said Mrs Coop.

She waited while Mrs Bamber whispered to the nurse. Then looking down the length of the aisle, Mrs Coop inspected the ward's linoleum.

'It's too bright!' she said. She wiped her eye: I can't see a thing with all this light. She dried her hand on her coat. 'I can't see if the floor's wet!' she added. Moving her cane, she took a step forward, then stopped to stare at the linoleum: it must be wet with all that shining. She took another step, then stopped to test the surface with the toe of her shoe: it seems all right. Shading her eyes, Mrs Coop stared at the linoleum.

'It's not wet is it?' she said, finally. She looked over her shoulder towards the reception desk and waited while Mrs Bamber continued whispering to the nurse. Then she eyed the wheelchair: after I nearly went over, they sat me there. They sat me there, and it mangled my hand when Dorothy pushed before I was ready.

Mrs Coop raised her voice:

'It's not *wet* is it?' she asked, and she repeated herself until Mrs Bamber put a finger to her lips.

Then Mrs Coop tapped the floor with the rubber knob at the end of her cane. 'I'm not slipping like last time. Remember, Dorothy, how I slipped last time when it was wet?' she said.

'No, it's not wet,' said the nurse. 'You won't slip.'

'I won't let you slip,' said Mrs Bamber. 'Just hang on, and I'll take you down in a minute.'

'Well, it's *shiny* like it's wet,' said Mrs Coop.

'It's just the polish,' said the nurse.

'Well, I'm not slipping on polish,' said Mrs Coop. 'I'm not slipping again and sitting in *that*,' she said, and she pointed at the wheelchair, then clenched her fist.

Mrs Bamber spoke to the nurse again. When she finished, she approached Mrs Coop, and taking her by the arm, she told her the news:

'The nurse agreed that Malcolm's cheeks are going rosy. Remember when I noticed yesterday that his cheeks were going rosy?' she said.

Mrs Coop observed the floor:

'I can't see a thing with this light,' she said. 'It's *dazzling*,' she added. Then she put a foot forward and stared down at her ankle. 'I feel it in the cold,' she said. 'My ankle feels *icy* in the cold.'

'Well, you'll soon warm up,' said Mrs Bamber. 'I'm roasting already!' She lowered her voice. 'I do get flushes now and again, you know with the change in life.' She wiped her forehead, then turned to speak to the nurse again while Mrs Coop leaned on her cane.

'No, it feels icy,' said Mrs Coop, and she flexed her hand, then repositioned her grip on the cane.

'What?' said Mrs Bamber.

'Cold: my ankle feels *cold*,' said Mrs Coop.

'Well, you'll soon be warm,' said Mrs Bamber. 'We'll sit you down next to that radiator by Malcolm's bed. You'll be warm as toast in no time!' she said.

'I don't like toast,' said Mrs Coop. 'A bit of plain bread does me just fine with some butter.'

'Yes, well, we can get something to eat later,' said Mrs Bamber, and she turned to speak to the nurse again. Then she squeezed Mrs Coop's arm. 'Are you all right?' she said.

As they walked, Mrs Coop's good eye teared in the sunlight:

'I can't see where I'm *going*!' she said.

'It's all right; just lean on me,' said Mrs Bamber.

After several steps, Mrs Coop stopped:

'You're going too fast,' she said.

'All right,' said Mrs Bamber, and they started off again. 'How's that?' she asked.

Mrs Coop eyed the linoleum:

'It's not wet is it?' she inquired.

'No,' said Mrs Bamber.

'Are we there yet?' asked Mrs Coop.

'No,' said Mrs Bamber.

Mrs Coop took a deep breath.

'Is Malcolm still asleep?' she asked.

'Yes,' said Mrs Bamber, 'but his cheeks are rosy, so that's an improvement: he's getting a bit of colour back.'

Pursing her lips, Mrs Coop focused on the linoleum:

'Is he a vegetable?' she asked.

'Of course, not,' said Mrs Bamber. 'I told you: his cheeks are rosy, so he's improving.'

'He's *ripening*,' said Mrs Coop. 'He's ripening like a *tomato*.'

'Just watch your step,' said Mrs Bamber.

Mrs Coop concentrated on the linoleum:

'It looks like Popsy's chess board, only green and white,' she said. 'I'm his Poppet,' she added. 'Popsy and Poppet, he used to say.'

'Shh,' said Mrs Bamber.

Then as they approached the tanned woman sitting with the stack of magazines in her lap, Mrs Bamber paused. 'Good morning,' she said. 'Isn't it lovely out?'

'Yes, it makes a change,' said the woman, and with one hand she reached to stroke the man lying in the bed next to her chair.

'It certainly does,' said Mrs Bamber, and she eyed the woman's gold jewellery, then continued to escort Mrs Coop down the aisle.

'It's like Popsy's chess board,' said Mrs Coop, and she looked up and asked Mrs Bamber. 'Is it four beds to go?'

'It's not so far,' said Mrs Bamber.

Then Mrs Coop stopped at the foot of the next bed:

'What's happened to him?' she asked as she looked at the empty bed.

'Who?' said Mrs Bamber.

'Him with the burns?' said Mrs Coop.

'I suppose they've moved him,' said Mrs Bamber. She tightened her grip on Mrs Coop's arm as she guided her forward. 'Isn't it a lovely morning, though?' she added.

After a moment, Mrs Coop stopped again:

'What's that noise?' she asked. 'It's *vibrating.*'

With her free hand, Mrs Bamber rotated the gold posts on her new earrings.

'I told you: it's road works just outside the entrance,' she said. 'That's why you smelled tar when we got out of the taxi.'

'Oh, right,' said Mrs Coop. She stepped forwards again. 'That's good for a cold,' she said.

'I know: you told me,' said Mrs Bamber.

'You inhale it right down; it's *warming*,' continued Mrs Coop, and she teetered sideways to avoid the hole in the linoleum.

'Just concentrate on your walking,' said Mrs Bamber, and she tightened her grip on Mrs Coop's arm.

When they reached the end of the ward, Mrs Bamber placed Mrs Coop's hand on the rail at the foot of the bed. Then rotating her earrings, she inspected the man in the next bed, and after she'd drawn the curtain between the beds, she dropped the blind in the window. Then she rolled the chair closer to the bed.

'See: he's getting his colour back,' she said. 'It's like I told you yesterday: his cheeks are definitely going rosy.'

'Well, they will do if he's ripening,' said Mrs Coop.

Mrs Bamber twisted the posts on her earrings. Then she removed a pillow from inside the bedside cabinet and placed it on the chair by the radiator. When she finished, she looked at the wall above the bed:

'Mr. Coup will come out of it any day now,' said Mrs Bamber as she read the name on the chart above his head. 'I mean, Malcolm,' she corrected.

Swaying slightly, Mrs Coop stared at her husband. Then she repositioned her cane so that it was off the green square of linoleum. When she finished, she looked at him again.

'He's smaller,' she said. 'He's definitely getting smaller.'

'Shall I help you with your coat?' asked Mrs Bamber.

'No,' said Mrs Coop. She listened. 'I told you,' she said, 'Malcolm's rasping when he breathes. '*Listen*!'

'He's just trying to say your name,' said Mrs Bamber, and she approached the end of the bed. 'You'll get too warm if you keep your coat on,' she added. 'It'll be an hour while I'm gone.'

With one hand, Mrs Coop stroked the front of her coat; then she stretched over the railing:

'Malcolm's toes curl lovely when he's sleeping,' she said.

'Well, what about your hat and gloves?' said Mrs Bamber, and she clasped Mrs Coop's outstretched hand, then guided her to the chair by the side of the bed, and after she'd hung Mrs Coop's cane on the bedside railing, she spoke again. 'Just let me help you,' she said as she removed Mrs Coop's hat and set it on the cabinet next to the bed. Then she bent forward and extending a hand, she started to remove Mrs Coop's gloves.

'No, my fingers are freezing!' said Mrs Coop, and she clenched her fists.

'I'll be gone an hour for the shopping,' said Mrs Bamber. 'Are you sure you don't want your gloves off as well?' She waited while Mrs Coop stared at the bags of fluid hanging from the stand on the other side of the bed. Then after a moment, she cleared her throat. 'Do you want a hand taking your *gloves* off?' she repeated, and she watched while Mrs Coop moved her lips. 'Yes?' said Mrs Bamber, and she bent forward again to remove a glove.

'No!' said Mrs Coop, and she clenched her fists again until Mrs Bamber took a step backwards. Then Mrs Coop pointed at the bags of fluid. 'What's that, then if it's not blood?' she asked.

'That's just to help him,' said Mrs Bamber. 'They want to keep his kidneys going. Now I'll just get your tape out. You can listen to it while I'm gone,' she said.

'Freddy Mampy had nice kidneys,' she said. 'Lamb and Ox. Lamb was best.'

Mrs Coop watched Mrs Bamber remove the cassette player from her handbag.

'Well, Malcolm's kidneys will definitely go if they give him all that. His bladder's only small these days,' said Mrs Coop. 'It's his prostate: it's *enlarged*,' she added, and she winced as she felt the cassette player drop onto her lap.

'Sorry about that,' said Mrs Bamber. 'Now will you be all right with your tape while I'm gone?' she asked. She rotated her earrings; then she waited. 'Now will you be all right with your tape while I'm gone?' she repeated.

Mrs Coop stared at her husband.

'I'll have to do something about the post,' she said.

'We can sort that out later today,' said Mrs Bamber.

'There might be a heating bill; the gas seems colder,' said Mrs Coop.

She watched Mrs Bamber twist her earrings.

'We'll go through it later, and I'll tell you what needs paying,' said Mrs Bamber.

'Oh, no,' said Mrs Coop, 'Malcolm wouldn't like that; it's *private*.'

'Well, we'll sort something out,' said Mrs Bamber, and she bent forward to pick up Mrs Coop's headphones. 'Do you want me to help you put these on before I go?' she asked.

'No, I'll be right,' said Mrs Coop, and she took her

headphones; then as she started to put them over her ears, Mrs Bamber stopped her.

'Is there anything else you want?' she asked. She lowered her voice. 'You don't have to go to the toilet, do you?'

Mrs Coop shook her head:

'Where's my pouch for my cassette player?' she asked.

'Well, you know where the toilet is if you need to go. Don't leave it too late; then you won't have to rush like last time,' said Mrs Bamber, and she reached to wipe a bread crumb from Mrs Coop's chin. 'I'll be back in an hour,' she added, 'and then we'll see about sorting that post out, all right?'

With both hands Mrs Coop pressed against her ears:

'But where's my medication tape?' she said. 'I can't hear it.'

Mrs Bamber helped Mrs Coop with her earphones; then she depressed the play button and waited until she heard the tape. 'Mind you don't have it too loud,' she said as she turned down the volume.

Shading her eye, Mrs Coop nodded.

'That's nice with the birds in the background. It's like spring singing,' she said.

Mrs Bamber held her finger up to her lip, then pointed at Mrs Coop's husband, and pursing her lips, Mrs Coop did the same as she watched Mrs Bamber step through the gap between the edge of the curtain and the wall.

When she'd gone, Mrs Coop glanced at her husband; then whispering, she began counting backwards: no, I forgot. I don't want Dorothy walking in on me again. I can never think what to say. She leaned forward in her chair and watched the gap between the floor and the edge of the curtain: well, there's no feet showing.

'Dorothy?' she said. 'Dorothy, are you there?' She waited, then felt along the side of her cassette player. 'Malcolm likes to hear my meditation tape,' she said, and she increased the volume, and as she listened, she leaned forward and stared at her husband's face: there's no movement. He wouldn't like to be a vegetable; of course, he's always had green fingers. She reached out to feel the edge of the mattress:

'Don't be so soft,' she said as she pressed against the blanket.

Then after several moments she leaned back in her chair, and listening, she stared at her husband's oxygen tube:

'I don't see how he breathes with that in his nose,' she said. She leaned forward: no, I can't see that machine where it goes. She leaned sideways and looked at the drips hanging from the stand on the other side of the bed: I told them I'd give blood if they wanted, but they said he was all right for that.

Squinting, she stared at the stain on the ceiling: I hope it's not. She shaded her eye: I hope it's not from someone's kidneys leaking through from above. She twisted in her chair to look out the window: no, it's the top floor we're on, I remember. It was when Jane Gawthorpe was in for her heart attack that there was a leak from the floor above: they were changing the plumbing. She frowned at the green blind in the window: no: it wasn't that: it was a strike. Everyone was on strike when Jane Gawthorpe had her heart attack. It was a three day week, and we'd no power half the time. She watched her husband's heart monitor: Malcolm missed his television. He listened to the radio instead. I always wondered why Popsy called it the wireless: when he got that kit, there was nothing but wires all over the back room.

She settled back in the chair, then looked up at the ceiling as she listened to the cassette tape: Dr. Bellum has a nice voice for teaching meditation. He sounds like Jimmy Young, only slower. He sounds like Jimmy Young with a *cold*. She closed her eye: that time

I sent Jimmy Young a card for his birthday, and he thanked me right on the air in the middle of his show. She yawned: I never had my name said on the radio before. She yawned again: it sounded nice the way he said it on the radio. Everyone thought it was very good of him…everyone but Freddy Mampy: he was furious because Jimmy Young said his name wrong, then made a joke out of mumpy and lumpy.

Mrs Coop smirked: it wasn't like in the old days when you had to come early, or you'd get nought. She pressed against her bladder: of course, we had next to nought to start off with back then. In those days it was mostly *offal*. Awful offal, we called it. Those were offal old days.

She grinned: of course, Freddy had his sign: *it pays to be an early bird*, and there was a drawing, only the early bird didn't have a worm; it had a sausage in its mouth. Mrs Coop licked her lips: and chalked on the sign next to the offal was a list of things we never had in the first place, and straight away, just as soon as we opened, Freddy would cross through them all and tell everyone we had sold out. Then he'd tell that joke of his. He was always telling it:

'There was this man who worked for a butcher. He was five foot ten inches tall, and he had one arm. What did he weigh?'

And Freddy would answer before any of us could:

'No: *meat*,' he'd say. 'He worked for a *butcher*.'

Freddy never tired of that.

Mrs Coop inspected the curtain surrounding the bed: it doesn't leave much for privacy with that gap practically up to your knees. If Malcolm was changing his pants, they could see. Of course, Malcolm isn't wearing any pants. She removed her earphones: that Dr. Bellum should just get on with the special breathing. Never mind all that business about scientific reasons. Watching her husband's heart monitor, Mrs Coop listened to his breathing: when

Dorothy took me back to the library, I told them I wanted that one about the loving hands, but they didn't have any Max Byegraves. Malcolm's always singing it.

She looked at the ceiling: of course, it was Bull Hill Hospital, not here, where we went to see Jane Gawthorpe when she had her heart attack. Mrs Coop pressed her earflaps closed: but that's gone now. So is Jane, bless her. Until then, I didn't think ladies could have heart attacks. Freddy Mampy said it was from walking her dog in the rain all those years. What she needed was a man and plenty of tripe, he said, and he gave his moustache a tweak. Mrs Coop lowered her hands: Freddy Mampy used to say that to all the ladies, but I always thought he fancied Polly. When he said it to her, she told him:

'If I had a man, that's all I'd have: plenty of *tripe*,' she said.

Mrs Coop wiped her mouth: Polly didn't like Freddy Mampy. Well, truth is, no one did, but Polly always had to make a point of it.

Mrs Coop put on her earphones. She looked at her husband and then at the wall in front of her: of course, you think Dr. Bellum's well-spoken until he says *home*. Even Mary Clegg knew not to drop her *h*'s; she always *over-said* them for Miss Armstrong.

She listened as she stared at her husband: at least we're at the end of the ward.

'At least we've got a wall to ourselves,' she said. She pressed her bladder. 'The toilet's handy as well, and there are no steps to climb, not like in our house,' she said, and she pressed her bladder again: no: I'm all right just yet. Rubbing her gloves together, Mrs Coop stared at the oxygen tube: they should put a dye in it, so you can see straight away if it's working. She wiped her eye, then concentrated on the cassette tape, and after several moments she frowned: if you think about saying *home*, you don't relax; you think of all the housework that needs doing.

Leaning forward, she touched the edge of the mattress, then withdrew her hand, placing it back on the cassette player: I can't reach him from here anyway. She looked at the radiator below the window: why do they always put radiators under windows? It's a waste of heat. Malcolm always says so when we go to dances at the Conservative Club. All he does between dances is go on about the radiators. He won't give over until the barman agrees with him that radiators under windows are a waste of heat.

'So why are you *wasting* heat in the *Conservative* Club?' he says.

Mrs Coop touched the radiator: if Malcolm could see all that heat escaping, he'd be fuming.

She dabbed her eye with the tip of her glove, then looked at her husband: it was there when we first met. She rubbed her eye: of course, Polly had seen Malcolm the week before, so she planned it all out: there was me and Polly and Jane Gawthorpe; then there was Malcolm and Bob Bash and that younger lad with the wispy moustache; we matched him up with Jane. Mrs Coop pinched her nose as she stared at her husband's oxygen tube: Dorothy says it's supposed to help him, but how can he breathe with that blocking his nose?

'It'd be worse than having a cold!' said Mrs Coop. Then she raised a finger to her lips, and turning her head towards the aisle, she stared at the gap under the curtain: I must stop that; I'll disturb the other patients, Dorothy says.

She removed her earphones and listened to her husband's breathing: I told Dorothy he's all raspy when he breathes, but she thinks he's trying to say my name:

'Elsie, do you hear that?' she says. 'He's saying it: El...*she*!'

Mrs Coop coughed: no, he's not: Aunt Aggie sounded like that as well. Of course, I wasn't speaking to Malcolm at the time.

'Just take her out and have her shot,' he said. 'That's what they do to animals in her condition. Well, just tie some antlers on her first and *then* have her shot,' he said.

Then Malcolm had her cremated when she wanted to be buried. She wanted to be buried in Birtwistle Cemetery just up the road. I could walk then and visit her each day, she said.

Malcolm knew, but he just blinked twice and denied it.

After removing her headphones, Mrs Coop placed the cassette player in her coat pocket; then she gripped the arms of her chair and concentrating, she stood stiffly on the linoleum, and as she looked down on her husband, she frowned: just trying to say my name? His rasping sounds nothing like *Elsie*. Aunt Aggie sounded just the same lying down with her emphysema. Mrs Coop stared at the oxygen tube, then removed a glove.

'Malcolm hates whiskers; he's forever shaving,' she said, and she touched the tip of his nose. Then she stared at the oxygen tube: so there was that one with the wispy moustache that we matched up with Jane Gawthorpe, and there was Bob Bash, and there was Malcolm. Polly fancied Malcolm at first, but just because of his height, she said. Mrs Coop looked up: I'd never known a girl as tall as Polly. She watched her husband's eyelashes: and while Polly was getting Bob Bash to ask me for a dance, Malcolm looked me straight in the eye, and he asked if I knew how to Lindy. Well, of course, I did. I wouldn't have been there if I didn't know how to Lindy.

Mrs Coop touched her husband's cheek as she stared at his eyelashes: Polly called them *come to bed eyelashes*.

'The way he batted them about. I bet you didn't even notice his dimples,' Polly said.

Mrs Coop smiled: of course, I noticed his dimples. I noticed everything about him but that patch of hairs on the end of his nose. It was only when he hadn't shaved that I noticed those. He'd been working all night, and he just dropped by to see me on his way back home.

'Your standards are slipping,' I said, and when I explained what I meant, he said I'd worn the same frock three days in a row. Well, I told him:

'It's not the same; it's a different scarf,' I said.

Yawning, Mrs Coop covered her mouth: it sends me to sleep, this meditating. She looked at the gap under the curtain: still not a foot in sight. It's not busy today, at least. She waited, then removed the cassette player from her pocket and set it on her husband's chest, and unblinking, she stared at his face as she stroked the wrinkle along his cheek: of course, before Aunt Aggie went, she could have been saying my name; she was awfully fond of me. She didn't have any children of her own.

Mrs Coop frowned: why don't they shave him? Malcolm always likes a shave; he's forever shaving. She rubbed her chin and looked at the radiator: they can waste heat putting radiators under windows, but they can't shave him. I'll ask Dorothy if there's a strike on.

'I'll tell her *we* should shave him,' she said, and she twisted her wedding band, then removed her headphones and placed them over her husband's ears.

'Of course, it wasn't called the Conservative Club when *we* met. It was called the Strawberry Duck back in those days,' she said, and as she stroked her husband's eyebrows, she started to hum. Then she stopped. 'And after the dance finished, I don't know where Polly or Jane Gawthorpe got off to, but Malcolm felt like a walk around town, so that's what we did.' She gripped the railing, then shifted her weight to the right: and when we got to the Co-op, he stopped and pointed. I'll never forget that:

'Those are the family's shops,' he said, and he pronounced the sign that way, but at that stage I didn't know his surname, did I?' she said.

She adjusted his headphones: he must be dreaming. He's always telling me about his dreams. It's because of me he dreams how his teeth fall out. It's enough to give *me* nightmares. She watched her husband's face:

'I bet you're dreaming about your buttered toast and Marmite,' she said; then she yawned. 'Of course, the Co-op's gone now,' she added, and she leaned more heavily on the railing. 'When they caught those lads who burned it down, remember how you wrote a letter to the paper?' She made her voice deep. '*It was disgraceful*, you said,' and she turned suddenly to her left:

'Are you all right?' asked the nurse as she drew back the curtain. Then before Mrs Coop could answer, the nurse looked back over her shoulder. 'I'm just coming,' she said.

'Yes, but you should shave him,' said Mrs Coop. Then her good eye widened as she fumbled to remove the headphones from her husband's ears and after she slipped the cassette player into her coat pocket, she watched the nurse attend to the woman visiting the patient in the bed across the aisle. Dorothy always says it's surprising they let her work here with that club foot.

'It's not inspiring to the patients,' Dorothy says.

When the nurse returned, she addressed Mrs Coop:

'Are you all right then?' she asked as she moved to the other side of the bed and started to unclip a bag from the hanger.

'But he needs those,' said Mrs Coop. 'He needs those for his kidneys. His bladder's only small these days; it's his prostate,' she explained.

'You're all right,' said the nurse. 'I'm just changing them before my shift ends.' She examined the bag. 'No, I'll just leave this one and make a note for Emma to change it when she comes in.'

Mrs Coop watched the nurse limp to her trolley, then return holding an empty bed bottle.

'Your daughter's just coming,' said the nurse as she stooped to reach beneath the bed.

'Will he know when my husband can come home?' asked Mrs Coop.

The nurse stood holding the old bottle, and as she read the amount, she frowned, then smiled at Mrs Coop before she stepped back to her trolley.

When the nurse had gone, Mrs Coop reached into her coat pocket and removed the cassette player. She pressed the play button, then set the cassette player on her husband's chest before she put her headphones over her ears. She listened: never shall I rest until my good gets better. She shook her head: at first I thought they said *butter*.

'And my better gets best,' she repeated.

Feeling for the edge of the mattress, she tugged on her husband's blanket: it's tucked in. She regarded his feet: the day I was doing the ironing when that pair of black pants appeared. They were so small, I thought they were one of his socks, but they were pants. After I realised what they were, I held them with a sock I'd just ironed.

She rubbed the patch on her eye: there was no y-front.

'Whose are these?' I asked.

Mrs Coop's face twitched.

'Whose are *these*?' I repeated.

She tugged at her husband's blanket.

'Mine,' he said.

She watched her husband's face: he hardly even looked up from his paper.

'Yours?' I said. 'Since when did you wear ladies' trollies?'''

'They're not *ladies',*' he said.

'Well, I know they're no *lady's*,' I said.

Then I told him there was no y-front.

'Well, they're *not* ladies',' he said.

'Well, they're not anything from Dunn's,' I said.

He shut his newspaper then and looked at me: that vein in his forehead was lumped up.

'I hate what you buy me from Dunn's,' he said, 'They're like *bloomers*!'

'Well, I'm not ironing *these*,' I said.

Then I tossed them at him, ironed sock and all.

Mrs Coop watched her husband's oxygen tube: he didn't say a word; he just dropped his newspaper onto the floor and stormed out of the room.

She listened, then covered her mouth: the nurse didn't say doctor; she said *daughter*. She thinks *Dorothy* is my daughter. Mrs Coop frowned: not wearing those red shoes, she isn't.

Feeling her bladder, Mrs Coop studied her husband's forehead: after he stormed out of the room, I followed, but before I could catch him up, he slammed the front door. He slammed it so hard, it bounced back open.

Mrs Coop's good eye narrowed as she stared at her husband: I'll never forget what he called me.

She blinked: then I saw Dorothy, and she pretended to be scrubbing her front step, but she must have heard him when he called me that before he drove away.

Mrs Coop pursed her lips: when he'd gone, I picked those pants up with the sock and hurled everything beneath the steps: the newspaper too.

Then after I cooked his tea, I waited: pork chops, it was.

She touched her forehead.

'I'm burning up,' she said, and she felt her cheeks, then prodded the glands in her neck. 'They say a hospital's the best place for catching bugs,' she said. She compared her two hands, then took her other glove off and felt her forehead again: that time I caught scarlet fever, and I had to go to the isolation hospital. It seems like only yesterday I was there.

She counted.

'It seems like only yesterday, but I was seven, in fact,' she said. She touched her forehead: I hadn't been on my own before, and there was only that glass window Popsy and Aunt Aggie could look through. They couldn't touch me: they weren't allowed.

Popsy and Poppet, she mouthed. That's what Popsy called me.

She watched her husband's heart monitor.

Polly said I should have been in hospital with that influenza, but Malcolm wouldn't hear of it. When I miscarried, Polly put it down to that, and so did Aunt Aggie. Of course, Malcolm didn't have to then, but he asked me anyway, and Aunt Aggie let us move back home when Polly told her I'd changed my surname.

She stared at her husband's oxygen tube: when he didn't come home, I worked myself up to it. I thought I might as well find out for sure, so I opened the curtain beneath the staircase. She clasped her hands over the bed rail: I'll never forget that sick feeling I had in my stomach: a *turning* when I picked up those pants; then I read the label: *men's large*, it said.

Mrs Coop flared her nostrils: well, I wondered: *what's a men's small like?*

She stared at her husband: he's definitely getting smaller. She pressed against her stomach: then after I ironed his regular pants, I ironed those black ones, but I didn't put them with his others. I put them with his socks instead.

'I'll give you better,' said Mrs Coop, and she unplugged the headphones, and as the cassette continued to play, she reached for her husband's oxygen tube.

'Elsie, I told you to keep quiet! I could hear you all the way down the aisle!' said Mrs Bamber.

Mrs Coop pinched harder on the oxygen tube. Then she let go and stood back as Mrs Bamber pressed the stop button on the cassette player.

'You're trouble, you are,' said Mrs Bamber.

Mrs Coop rubbed her nose.

'You're not my daughter, not in those red shoes, you're not,' she said, and she pointed at Mrs Bamber's stilettos. 'You look like that Willacy girl wearing those,' she said, and as she teetered backwards, Mrs Bamber reached for her coat sleeve, then helped to lower Mrs Coop back into the armchair by the side of the bed.

Six

Upstairs in her bathroom, Mrs Coop listened to the fan: it'd deafening, that. You can hear it from outside whirring for *ages* after. She pressed her bladder: I always go with the light out if I can. It must have been Malcolm. No, the seat's not up. It must have been Dorothy. She was in a hurry to get the washing in before the bin men came.

Listening, Mrs Coop flushed the toilet, and while she watched the new water run in, she adjusted her husband's bifocals, then pressed her bladder and stepped sideways towards the sink to regard herself in the mirror: there's not another one like it, the widower said when he gave this coat to Aunt Aggie. He said the stripes make zebras practically invisible. She pulled the cowl over her head and turned her face from one side to the other as she watched herself in the mirror: it's *blinkering*. Aunt Aggie always said so when she wore it. Mrs Coop touched her eye patch: of course, I can't see from that side anyway.

She sniffed, then made a sour face: Aunt Aggie's coat stinks of mothballs. I saw her taste a mothball once. She thought they were sweeties. She was getting on then. Of course, I didn't tell Malcolm. He was always looking for excuses.

As she watched the extractor fan, she covered her ears, and listening, she pressed harder against the zebra skin: I can still hear that fan. She uncovered her ears, then scratched her palms: when Malcolm first put it in, I told him I didn't like it.

'The whole street can hear it going around. Now everyone will know when we're on the toilet. It goes on for ages after,' I said.

Regarding herself in the mirror, Mrs Coop listened: well, it was just him being fussy when he first retired.

'We're not seedlings; we won't damp off,' I said.

She looked up at the ceiling: besides, it was only a tiny bit of plaster that fell on him.

Mrs Coop looked down at the sink, then pulled back a sleeve, and listening, she stared at her wrist: I feel naked without my watch. I never got a gold one working for Freddy Mampy. She looked at her wrist again, then turned to leave, and as she stepped forward, she bumped against the side of the bath: Dorothy told me Malcolm can't eat anything proper, but they should at least shave him twice a day. He likes shaving. Through the zebra skin, Mrs Coop rubbed her knee: I don't know how to, or I'd do it myself. She observed the ring around the inside of the bath: it was always Aunt Aggie who shaved Popsy when he wasn't so well.

She looked up at the cluster of patterned tiles: that time Malcolm added the shower to the bath, I was always lowering it; he was always raising it. It was up and down like a yo-yo, so in the end I told him I wanted rid of it. It was him who chose the fruit basket tiles.

'Those are kitchen tiles,' I said.

But he insisted: they were on *sale*.

Mrs Coop blinked twice.

'I'll ask Dorothy if she knows how to shave him,' she said. Then she shook her head. 'Not unless he tells me where my savings stamps are,' she added. 'I keep telling him they're worthless without me: they're not transferable; it's printed on them in red.'

Standing upright, she adjusted her brassiere, and on her way out the door, she pulled the cord to the light switch, then paused when the light clicked off: I can still hear that fan whirring: it's even *squeaking* these days. She listened: Fee's ear would perk right up at that mousy sound it's making.

Mrs Coop flexed her hand: they'll have records at D'Radcliffe's. They'll know it was me who bought them, not Malcolm. They're useless to him. She stepped forward, then stopped in front of the door to the back bedroom: I forgot my handbag. She turned around, and when she felt inside the bathroom door, she gripped the cord and pulled. Then she stepped forward, and listening to the tap drip, she looked into the sink at her handbag: it'll be wet with that; I shouldn't have put it there.

After shaking water off the leather, she examined herself in the mirror: I had my doubts, but the widower explained how they blend in like chameleons with stripes. Then he told us about shooting the zebra when he was in Africa, and he showed me the head on the wall that Aunt Aggie was always going on about.

'See,' she said, 'it's got glass eyes.'

Then the widower interrupted Aunt Aggie's story, and he explained again how you can't see a zebra from far away with its stripes.

Mrs Coop frowned, then turned to leave: well, you can't see anything from far away. It's nothing down to stripes.

On her way out, she touched the shower tiles, then blew on her fingers:

'I told Malcolm his new tiles are too cold,' she said, and she stepped out of the bathroom, then looked into her bedroom: I never liked that wardrobe: it crowds the room. It crowds the room, *and* it's half empty. She sniffed: it was all right in Aunt Aggie's room, but hers is bigger than ours.

After moving past her bedroom, Mrs Coop rested her hand on the wallpaper. She waited, then patted her handbag, and stepping sideways, she gripped the banister while she looked down the staircase: it's rippling, that raspberry carpet, only it's plum. She frowned: it's rippling down to Fee's step. Teetering, she gripped the banister again, then studied the doorway to her left: I'll just have another look out front before I go.

When she stepped inside the room, she gazed at the unmade bed. We sold my bed after we were married. She scanned the room: it's bigger, this room, with just the one bed. Feeling the headboard, Mrs Coop jiggled the bed, then moved towards the bay window: these floorboards are always creaking. You could hear Aunt Aggie pacing when she got up with her indigestion. She was glued to our window when she wasn't pacing; then when Popsy came home, she'd have a go at him for waking her up.

Feeling for the windowsill, Mrs Coop looked down at the aspidistra, then set her handbag next to it: I haven't missed Dorothy, have I? After lifting a sleeve, she looked at her wrist: I don't know. She dropped the sleeve; then with one hand, she curled a leaf on the aspidistra as she considered her husband's Ford Anglia. I told him it was the same turquoise as that Indian jewellery Polly used to send. He wanted black, but I told him black was for hearses. Mrs Coop regarded the sunroof: he calls it a sunroof, but it's always leaking! I asked him when he fit that:

'Why do you need a sunroof when it's always raining?'

She held out her hand as she looked at the sky: well, it's *nearly* always raining. She arched her back: this coat was too big for Aunt Aggie as well. When she wore it with her hood up, Malcolm called her the Grim Reaper.

'I'll reap you,' she said.

Mrs Coop rubbed her backside: with that sunroof leaking, my seat's always wet when we go to the crematorium. It's embarrassing. I tell Aunt Aggie how things are getting on; then I have to explain why Malcolm stayed in his car again.

'It's his radio: he's afraid someone will *steal* it,' I say.

But Aunt Aggie knows.

Mrs Coop pursed her lips: that time we had those gales from the hurricane, I wondered: did Aunt Aggie blow away?

Mrs Coop considered the clouds: Malcolm didn't think so. He didn't think so, but he didn't see her plot after. He just stayed in his car, guarding his radio. All the plots were in a right state, and there were ashes all over the lawns. Mrs Coop shrugged her shoulders: when I got back to the car, I kept telling him:

'It looked more like the Garden of Eternal *Unrest*,' I said, but he was only interested in his football scores. He kept repeating the results after the announcer said them:

'Them winning's not so good for us,' he'd say.

She scanned the length of her husband's car: you'd think he'd worry more about someone stealing all his chrome. He's forever polishing it. I tell him:

'How about polishing Aunt Aggie's silver tea set while you're at it?'

She shaded her eyes, then focusing on the bonnet, Mrs Coop regarded the coat hanger: he's been meaning to fix that for months. With both hands she flipped the edges of the cowl away from her face: it stinks of mothballs *and* it scratches. She rubbed her cheeks: *and* it weighs a tonne. It weighs as much as a zebra.

Touching the window, Mrs Coop looked up the street at the man in the dark suit. He's knocking: it's not Sunday. It's not those Witnesses. They wouldn't come on a bin day would they? She regarded the next house down: there's another! They must be selling something; I don't know what. She removed her husband's bifocals: I told Malcolm I can see better without them. Her good eye watered as the car approached: speak of the devil. She took a step backwards: It's not come for him in number sixteen? He's not been so well. Red shoes? She blew air from the corner of her mouth. It's not a hearse; it's a taxi! It's Dorothy with her taxi; she *never* takes a bus. Mrs Coop pulled back a sleeve and tapped her wrist:

'No, it's in the shop,' she said.

She creaked across the floorboards, and when she emerged from the bedroom, she paused to stare at the carpet, then continued to the landing, and when she reached it, she gripped the banister, then stepped down with her good foot.

'Eleven,' she said, and counting, she stepped down again.

I always like going down that double staircase in D'Radcliffe's: it makes me feel like her in those films with Fred Astaire. I'd give my eye teeth for D'Radcliffe's winding staircase. They can keep their spinning doors, though; they're like that waltzer at Blackpool: each time I got on, I'd think I'll never get out of my teacup.

When Mrs Coop reached the third step from the bottom, she rested: it's not rippling, but burgundy's nice for a carpet. She shook her head: Malcolm wanted to skin Fee alive when he saw what she'd done to the carpet. She tested the carpet with the toe of her shoe: well, Fee didn't mean to ruin it; she was only scratching.

'I'd skin *him* first, I said,' and she nodded, then crossed herself as she turned her face towards the ceiling. 'I'm not religious, but there's no harm in it,' she said. She touched the wallpaper: they're comforting, my pagodas. With her thumbnail, she pressed into the embossment, then looked down at the carpet. 'Naughty puss!' she said.

She gripped the banister: Malcolm wouldn't give over:

'That fur of hers will do nicely for a step!' he said, and he'd got that carving knife out.

Mrs Coop shook her head: but I wouldn't let him:

'I'd skin *him* first,' I said.

She consulted her watch: no! She studied the steps remaining, then moved down.

'Two!' she said, and she stepped down again.

When she reached the bottom, she lifted the cowl off her cheeks and turned to look up the staircase: it's been a long while since I've slid down that banister. She shaded her eyes: the last time was with Mary Clegg. Her folks were away, so she was staying over, and she knocked her front tooth out sliding down the banister. Mrs Coop pressed a finger against her lip: it was only a milk tooth, but Popsy forbid us from doing it again. She tapped her front tooth: before Aunt Aggie moved in, we were nothing short of animals, she always said.

Mrs Coop studied the edge of the coat sleeve, then looked up at the ceiling rose: when the priest said Aunt Aggie's name at the funeral, it didn't sound right. She shrugged her shoulders: even Malcolm agreed: *Prudence Agatha* didn't sound right. He agreed it made her sound like some old *prunes*. He agreed but he didn't get out of his car. Mrs Coop adjusted her brassiere, then felt for the cane hooked over the end of the banister. Not even on my first visit, he wouldn't leave his radio. I had to find Aunt Aggie's plot on my own. She shrugged her shoulders, then headed for the kitchen.

As she neared the telephone table, she paused: no, I'm not to touch it. Dorothy says they'll make me pay. She stepped forward, and after she closed the refrigerator door, she stared at the magnetic maple leaf; then she examined the map: well, someone from over there should be able to read it. She glanced at the toaster, then moved past the gas hobs, and when she reached the back door, she examined her wrist: I better hurry, or they'll have been and gone.

She opened the door, then stepped out into the back yard: Dorothy still complains about the bin men coming on wash day. Mrs Coop avoided the crack between the paving slabs: she complains, but she won't do her washing on another day, not like me.

'Well, you always have Sunday off,' Malcolm said, and he started calling it *Sud*-day.

Mrs Coop stumbled.

She stopped to scowl at the broken paving stone, then prodded the corner of it with her cane.

'I told Malcolm to fix that.'

When she reached the privy, she opened the door and stepped inside: it's stinking. Malcolm's meals are stinking. Breathing through her mouth, she picked up the black bin liner, and as she stood in the doorway of the privy, she inspected the back of Mrs Bamber's house, then stepped forward: she hasn't seen me yet, not with this coat on.

When Mrs Coop reached the gate at the end of her yard, she stopped: I better hurry. She set the bin liner on top of the coal bunker, and with her right hand, she reached out and pressed against the gate: I better hurry, or they'll have been and gone. She hung her cane on her right arm, and with her left hand freed, she pressed down on the latch, then pulled the gate towards her: no. She looked at her right hand: maybe he's locked it from the outside? I'll have to go round the other way then.

Mrs Coop's head bobbed as she let go of the latch and stared at the gate: there's no *time* if I go around the other way! She stared at the gate, then reached forward: of course: he's put the latch on to keep the kids out of the yard. With both hands, Mrs Coop slid back the latch, then pulled the gate towards her. When it was open, she took the cane off her right arm, and leaning on it, she picked up the bin liner, and as she passed through the gate, her elbow brushed against the bricks.

She looked to her right and then to her left:

'They're gone!' she said. She closed her eye, then opened it and looked again. 'The bins are gone!' Leaning on her cane, Mrs Coop stood near the edge of the gutter that ran down the centre of the alley: what time is it? She curled her lip: well, I can't see with my hands full.

'They must have taken them down to the end,' she said. She listened: they must have taken them down quietly. 'Usually it's nothing short of thunder when they move the bins,' she said.

Mrs Coop followed the gutter: I'll have to hurry. They only move them just before they come. When she reached the first line of laundry, she stopped and stared at the sheet billowing in front of her: well, I'll never get through that. She looked down the line of the laundry, then moved to the right until she reached the section of black socks, and stooping beneath them, she took a step forward, then gasped. When she'd steadied herself with the cane, she looked down at the flattened egg carton:

'That could have been the death of me,' she said, and she scowled at the rotten gate to the house next door. She raised her voice. 'Of course, these days no one looks after things if they're renting.'

She listened: that sounds like them coming up Devon Street. I better put my skates on. After she made her way through the next three rows of laundry, she stopped.

'It's no good rushing these days. I can't *breathe*!' she said. She glanced at the skip, then stared at the soapy water running down the iron grate in the gutter: it'll be him in number two, Devon, washing his car. He always washes his car on Monday. He parks it out back at the top to make it awkward for Winifred to put out her washing.

Mrs Coop cringed, then looked up at the sky: I *hate* aeroplanes: they're worse than falcons screeching. She listened: it's pipping, that reversing. With her cane, she parted the sheets, and after she stepped through, she stopped and looked towards the end of the alley.

'There they are,' she said. 'At least I'm not too late.'

She started to move the cane forward, then looked down at the grate: not stuck! Mrs Coop twisted the cane free, then continued forwards, and when she reached the bins, her face twitched as she peered to read the numbers: eight? She took two steps forward: no: three. She looked to her left: nothing on that one. She looked to her right:

'Devon?' She read the next bin. 'Devon! These aren't even our street's!' she said. She looked behind her. 'Ours must be at the other end!' She regarded the bin liner: it's Malcolm who looks after the bin; he never said anything about it going to one end or the other when he fetches it back. She examined the bin in front of her: I'll just have to put it in one of these. After regarding the front of her coat, she scanned the overlooking windows, then set the bin liner down on top of the next nearest Wheelie bin before she lifted the lid to number eight: at least it's not full. Pursing her lips, she considered first the bin liner, and then the hand gripping her cane, and then the hand holding open the lid: I'd have to be an octopus! I told Malcolm what I could do with is one of those canes with four legs that stands up on its own.

She cringed: it's those breaks on the bin lorry; they're *hissing*! Mrs Coop dropped the lid: what *am* I thinking? Someone might find it! She looked up at the windows: they'll tell Dorothy I'm not eating, and she'll tell Doctor Khan. It'll be like that time I didn't take his tablets, and I had to have injections instead. Well, a horse, couldn't swallow his tablets, a zebra couldn't. She listened to the bin lorry: I better make a move! As she turned to pick up the bin liner, her ankle cracked.

'Turnips!' she said, and while she waited for the pain to ebb, Mrs Coop's eyes watered; then she shook her head. 'I can't wait! They're coming!' she said, and she picked up the bin liner and started to hobble along the first line of laundry until she came to a parting in the sheets. Then as the breaks hissed on the bin lorry, Mrs Coop pushed her way through, then limped towards the brick wall. When she reached it, she turned, and with her back leaning against the wall, she watched the bin men through the gap between the wall and the sheet: I feel like those Local Defence Volunteers.

'Look, duck, and *vanish*,' she said, and she glanced down at her coat. 'I don't think they saw me, anyway,' she whispered. Then she regarded the tarmac patch in the cobbles: when they finally dug up those lead pipes, Malcolm wrote to the Council. He wasn't bothered by drinking the water; he wanted reimbursement for the lead.

'That pipe was ours,' he said. 'The Council had no business carting it away lining their own pockets.'

Suddenly, Mrs Coop lunged forward onto her cane:

'Sugar!' she said. 'Turnips!'

'I'm sorry, luv. Are you all right?' said the woman. She looked at Mrs Coop. 'I didn't knock you over did I?' she asked, and she opened the gate wider, then humped a kitchen unit into the skip.

Mrs Coop blinked: no: no I don't recognise her: she must be *new*. She must be the one with three cars that Dorothy was on about.

'Devon Street's full up with all of their cars,' she said.

Mrs Coop rubbed her right elbow as she stared at the skip:

there's nothing wrong with those cabinets. It's a shame to thrown them.

'Are you all right?' asked the woman.

After several moments, Mrs Coop answered:

'I'm not so bad,' she said.

'You can put that in our skip,' said the woman, and she indicated the bin liner.

Mrs Coop turned scarlet as she limped down the alley. Before she passed through the next line of washing, she stopped and looked over her shoulder, and when she saw that the woman was still watching, she ducked unsteadily beneath the mini skirt: I hope she hasn't seen me going into that bin from Devon Street. Reeling forward with her cane, Mrs Coop hurried to reach her back gate: they should have replaced the tarmac with cobbles, or they should have tarmaced the whole alley.

'It's a right bodge job,' Malcolm says.

She opened the gate, then stepped inside, and after she shut the gate, she slid the latch forward: Malcolm would be pleased: he's always going on about me leaving things. Well, it wasn't *me* who got the car aerial broken: he forgot to put it down when he parked it in town, and we've never been in the new multi-storied car park since. As her stomach rumbled, she studied the neighbouring windows before she opened the door to the privy and stepped inside.

'I forgot to check for spiders first,' she said, and she set the bin liner next to the tea chest.

Seven

Mrs Coop parted the curtain in the front room. She chewed an indigestion tablet and peered out the bay window: it's dark. Fee's rose looks freezing in the lamplight. She sucked pieces of the tablet, then closed the curtain: I don't like to think of Fee out there in the cold; it's stiffening.

Turning, she considered the post divided on the sofa: it's only bills since Christmas. She massaged the fingers on her left hand: I told Dorothy it's Malcolm who writes the cheques, not me. Mrs Coop swallowed the tablet: except for that time on his fiftieth when I surprised him with the rotovator. Here's me not knowing about that Willacy girl. She cracked a knuckle: Cyril was in on it. He delivered the rotovator to Malcolm's allotment, and Malcolm hadn't the slightest inkling.

She shook her head at the antimacassar on her husband's armchair: I wouldn't have bothered, if I had known; I'd have bought him something for the house instead: a paintbrush. Rubbing the smudge of ink from the side of her hand, Mrs Coop looked at her husband's photograph next to the armchair: he was late when he got back, but when he came in, he was humming his song about the hands to love you. When I smelled his breath, I told him he was late:

'Your gooseberry pie is burned,' I said.

He kept humming. He showed me his dirty hands:

'Take no notice,' he said, and then he showed me how the rotovator worked. He acted it out with the different speeds and positions. He was all over the back room making his rows. He got carried away with it being his birthday.

'How about that restaurant next to Cyril's shop?' he said. 'You're only fifty once. I bet they do gooseberry pie up there.'

I told him:

'It's *Greek*. You never eat foreign. You don't *like* it.'

Mrs Coop cracked another knuckle: well, we didn't eat out. He didn't want to really, so I salvaged the pie: I scraped it off, then painted the crust again with egg white and sprinkled the sugar. She glared at her husband's photograph: then he was so tipsy, he didn't even notice what I'd done. All he went on about was the new potatoes he'd grown. Well, it wasn't the new potatoes; it was the butter he liked. She scrutinised her husband's photograph:

'Malcolm,' she said, 'My D'Radcliffe's savings stamps are not transferable. They're worthless to you.'

Mrs Coop turned her back to the photograph, and prodding the ache in her stomach, she considered the sofa: no, I never hid them there.

Shivering, she stepped out of the front room and into the hallway, and when she reached the mirror, she stopped to put on her husband's bifocals; then stepping forward, she bumped into the wall: I tell him, but he insists:

'At least they'll protect your eyes,' he says.

She moved the bifocals to the tip of her nose; then peering over the rims, she opened the door to the back room and sniffed: I should have lit the fire; it's freezing. She scanned the room: after Popsy went, Aunt Aggie kept seeing him. One night she saw him out back, feeding his pigeons. Mrs Coop inspected the two chairs in front of the gas fire: I told her she was going daft, but the next night she woke me up, and there was no denying it: there *was* the smell of pipe smoke in Popsy's bedroom. Inhaling, Mrs Coop flared her nostrils: and Popsy *never* smoked in there. She exhaled: of course, I told Aunt Aggie it was left over from his clothes:

'Pipe smoke's terrible for clinging,' I said.

But she wouldn't give over:

'No, he's hanging about,' she said. 'He's still here, and if feeding his pigeons isn't proof there's life after, I don't know what is!'

Aunt Aggie insisted she saw him.

Mrs Coop stepped into the back room, and when she reached the two chairs by the fire, she felt the leatherette; then when she touched the cushion on the rocking chair, she jerked back her hand: it's eerie. She looked behind her:

'Malcolm?' she whispered.

She shook her head: I remember when we first put carpet in the bedroom, I could hardly get Aunt Aggie's chair to rock.

'You did set your mind on the highest pile. What did you expect?' Malcolm said.

He wanted to move it, but I liked looking out onto the back gardens in Devon Street, so he put that sheet of something hard for me to rock on.

'This way you won't make grooves in the carpet,' he said. 'I'm not paying for the highest pile and then watch you make grooves in it.'

Nodding, she stood up, then rubbed the small of her back: when I see Malcolm, I'll tell him. She bent forward, then felt each seat again:

'Mine's definitely warmer,' she said, 'I'll tell him to sit in his own chair if he's haunting.' She frowned at the rocking chair. 'Well, I'll tell him not to sit in Aunt Aggie's.' She looked at the window, then regarded the kitchen table beneath it. 'I'm sure I pushed that chair in,' she said.

She crossed the room and looked down at the meal: after they delivered the first one, I told Dorothy:

'They're all divided up; everything's in its own place like in Malcolm's allotment. He'd like that,' I said. 'Of course, he'd *prefer* it in rows,' I added.

After several moments, Mrs Coop picked up the fork, and whispering, she prodded the ring on top of the gammon: no, it's set solid. She removed her husband's glasses and stared at the pink centre, then prodded again.

'It's not an egg; it's one of those pineapples!'

She set the fork, then the knife, and then the spoon diagonally across the tray. Then gripping the tray with both hands, Mrs Coop carried the uneaten meal back to the kitchen, and humming, she scraped it into the pressure cooker, then dropped the tin tray into the sink before she stepped to the refrigerator and opened the door.

Sniffing, she stared at the jar of Marmite, then scanned the rest of the fridge: I threw those radishes, didn't I?…didn't I? They give me indigestion. She stooped to open a vegetable drawer: just that prize turnip. She shut the drawer, then opened the one next to it and felt inside: no, not here either. She took a deep breath as she pushed the vegetable drawer closed: I must clean that out one day. I thought I'd thrown the brussel sprouts and the beet root. She stepped backwards, then closed the refrigerator door, and pausing, she stared at the magnetic maple leaf: there's Polly's map. I never could make heads nor tails of it. She squinted: well, it's not in English.

She re-opened the refrigerator door: I better have a look, just in case. Sucking the insides of her cheeks, Mrs Coop lifted first the butter and then the egg flap: that time he grew the prize gooseberries, he kept them there for weeks. Swallowing, she stared at the jar of Marmite, then gripped it, and with one hand she shut the refrigerator door, and her good eye widened as she positioned the Marmite on the countertop to cover the burn mark: Malcolm could have fired the house with that cigar. She lit the gas ring on the cooker, then frowned: no, I don't want tea; it's his buttered toast and Marmite. I tell him Marmite just spoils the butter. Her stomach rumbled as she turned off the gas.

'All right, I'm just coming,' she said, and she opened the bread bin. 'What's the time?' she asked, and she looked at her wrist: I keep forgetting my watch is in the shop.

She put bread in the toaster; then after she lifted the cover from the plate of butter, she clutched the jar of Marmite, and holding the lid still, she twisted the bottle against the countertop: when I found Fee, she was flat; she looked more like a rug than a cat:

'Fee!' I said.

Mrs Coop frowned: and when I kissed her, there was that new smell, not the smell from her licking, not the smell from the vet's when he trimmed the cancer off her ear. That's when I called Malcolm.

As the Marmite began to twist open, Mrs Coop's stomach rumbled: I looked, and at first I saw nothing but a tea towel. Then reaching for that, I remembered my apron next to the fridge. When the lid dropped onto the countertop, Mrs Coop blinked, then looked at the peg where her apron used to hang. I called Malcolm. I called him again and again. Mrs Coop shook her head: it seemed like an eternity, and when he finally did come down, there wasn't a stitch on him.

'Malcolm,' I said, 'put on your clothes!'

She looked at the back door: but he wouldn't budge.

Mrs Coop turned her hand palm upwards and concentrated against the cramp. Instead of going for his clothes, he reached for my apron. He snatched it from Fee; then he wrapped my apron around his middle like a bath towel. I told him not to. I told him my apron was for Fee, but he took no notice.

She concentrated, and slowly, her fingers started to open: my blue apron with the white stripes. She stared at the red imprint the lid had made on the palm of her hand. Then he shouted; he ordered *me* to go and get his clothes, and he didn't even notice Fee; he was so busy watching the back door, so then I looked, and there was the Willacy girl from Devon Street.

Mrs Coop closed her good eye.

After several moments, she opened her eye. She rubbed it, then stared at the back door. Of course, Malcolm replaced the clear glass then with the frosted ferns, but it was too late; that was the start of it. That was the start of it with that *bicycle*! Sniffing, she opened the cutlery drawer: the next day we bought Fee's rose and buried her beneath it. Well, I cried the whole way there: I cried like a baby: floods.

She pressed her fingertips against the prongs of a fork: well, I didn't want to go out so soon after, but he insisted. Moving her hand further to the right, she felt the spoons, then the knife blades: he had those special passes; he didn't want to waste them. Mrs Coop set the knife next to the jar of Marmite: the vet said whoever did it could be charged with *cruelty*! We put up notices, but nothing ever came of it. She opened a cupboard and removed a plate.

'It's *only* a cat,' Malcolm said, and he read me his special passes.

Mrs Coop watched the toaster: well, he and Fee never did get on. She set the plate next to the knife; then she put the knife diagonally on top of the plate: when we got there, it was sweltering, and Malcolm made a big to do about his passes: they allowed him to park up front.

'Look,' he said, 'we're right next to the entrance.'

Mrs Coop sucked her cheeks as the toast popped up.

'It's only some old field. How can a field have an *entrance*?' I said.

She swallowed, but he kept on reading; he explained how his special passes would get us into the hospitality tent, and I told him I wasn't ill, just grieving. Mrs Coop pressed her stomach: I didn't get out of the car at first; I was wrenching with grief: Fee was only a cat. She was only a tabby. How could they?

Mrs Coop swallowed.

'Smarten yourself up,' he said, and he put his seat back and read out loud from the pamphlet until I told him I wasn't interested in growing bigger vegetables than I ever dreamed of.

'I never dream of vegetables, big *or* small,' I said.

Then he offered me a Polo mint and adjusted the air freshener, a little pine tree, it was, and after that he opened the glove compartment and polished his radio with that special rag. Not made from his old shirts cut up like I use, but a special rag; I asked him what it was: it looked something like leather from that chair of his, and when he blinked twice and got out of the car, I knew he was lying about getting his rag from work.

Mrs Coop felt in each pocket of her cardigan: no: no tissue. She removed the toast with a tea towel, then spread the toast with butter: I got out of the car eventually. Well, I had to: they'd given him two ice creams from that tent, and they were *melting*! She stared at the jar of Marmite: while we ate the ice creams, we watched the goldfish in the pond just inside the entrance. Mrs Coop shook her head: not *goldfish*.

'Those aren't goldfish; those are carp: *coy carp*,' he said.

Then he fed the carp his cone, and when he dropped a handful, all the pieces disappeared instantly. I told him:

'It looks like the water's *boiling*!' I said.

Mrs Coop felt for the glasses on the chain around her neck, and after she put them on, she concentrated, but her fingers clutched twice too soon as she moved her hand towards the Marmite. She frowned: I didn't think those carp were shy at all; they were just plain *greedy*.

'They'll bite you,' I said. 'They're worse than those ducks always biting children's fingers at your park.'

She removed the glasses, and after she picked up the knife, she buttered the toast again.

'Carp don't have any teeth,' he explained. 'See, they only suck,' he said, and he bent down and let one suck the last piece of cone off the end of his finger.

Gripping the toast, Mrs Coop mixed the Marmite with the butter: the sight of it made my skin crawl: all rubbery-lipped it was; I'll never forget: orange with black speckles.

'He always has it too thick,' she said.

She set the toast on the plate and continued spreading Marmite until the butter blackened: it's like treacle. She cut the toast into soldiers, then positioned the pieces one by one on the plate. She licked her fingers and sniffed the end of the knife as she stepped to the sink.

After she cleaned the knife, she turned off the tap, and dried her hands on the tea towel. Then she stepped backwards until she felt the countertop against the small of her back, and staring at the cat flap in the back door, she rested against the simulated marble:

of course, it's ages since he finished with the Willacy girl, but it seems like yesterday. She curled a lip at the empty jar on the windowsill next to the sink: I *was* warned. Aunt Aggie said so after he brought me home from the dance.

'He's a looker,' she said. 'Get yourself something plain and sensible.'

Mrs Coop shook her head at the empty jar: each year Malcolm prunes Fee's rose, but it always grows back just as big: *gi-normous* and full of blossom. I showed Malcolm the label: scarlet red, it said; only the blossoms turned out to be white. She flared her nostrils: when you open the window, you can smell Fee's rose. He complains, but it doesn't block out the light. It's his car that blocks out the light.

'It's bloody typical: when that cat was alive, it sprayed everything I ever planted. It made a point of it. It *lived* for it. Now just look at the size of that rose!'

She grinned: that time Fee killed all those pots of something Malcolm was growing secretly for one of his competitions.

'I'll not risk keeping these at the allotment,' he said.

Well, he should have done: she was straight onto them.

Mrs Coop glanced at the frosted window in the back door, then stared at the cat flap: *he*, I mean. With the knuckle of her index finger, she touched the corner of her good eye. We only found out when we took Fee in to have that cancer trimmed off her ear. She'd been scratching it for ages, but I thought it was just a flea she had. Mrs Coop's stomach rumbled: *he*, I mean…cats are always girls to me, though.

She turned to face the back door: when Fee came back, she was lopsided; her left ear was *twice* as big as her right. Mrs Coop shook her head: she never walked straight after that, but she still played with her catnip mouse…that poor catnip mouse, she did nothing but maul it. Fee'd been done anyway, the vet said, but Malcolm swore after that, Fee started spraying.

Supporting herself with her right hand on the countertop, Mrs Coop stepped forward until she reached the light switch on the back wall. Then resting, she stared at the door: frosted ferns now, but I can't see a thing through it. She peered through the pattern: I can't even see my bird feeder. She drummed her fingers on the glass: all those years we could never feed the birds, and now I can't even see it: all because of that *bicycle*.

She switched on the outside light: when I walked in on him, he was sitting in Aunt Aggie's rocking chair, and he wasn't rocking, he was watching that Willacy girl through our bedroom window. She was in their kitchen doing the washing up.

'Just like that monkey in the zoo with it,' I said, and the next day I had him move Aunt Aggie's rocking chair downstairs.

Mrs Coop rapped the glass: he never put any of his frosted glass in our bedroom window, though. She looked at the jar on the windowsill: there's no flower. When he apologises, he always brings a flower. Just the one, though. He never brings me more than one.

Mrs Coop shook her head. Then looking down at the cat flap, she shivered: it's still draughty, Fee's flap.

She pointed at the door:

'Make the hole on the right,' I said, but he did it on the left. I told him not to because of the sink.

He took me outside: from *there* it was on the right.

'But the sink: I said *away* from the sink.'

'No, you didn't,' he said, and he blinked his eyes together twice like that.

Mrs Coop stared at her reflection in the frosted glass: everyone knew about him and that Willacy girl. She inspected the tin tray in the bottom of the sink: even *I* knew. With her left hand she reached to turn on the tap, and after several seconds the water spurted out, splashing her arm.

Flexing her bicep, Mrs Coop stared until she felt the water soak through to her skin: it used to be muscle, then fat, then flab, then what did he call it? She waited, watching the water spatter onto the tray. He didn't need to blink: I *knew*. She picked the jar off the windowsill and filled it with water.

'Enough,' she said, and she set the jar down on the coaster.

Then her hand slipped when she turned the tap backwards: bat wings: *that* was what he called it. She shook her head: everyone knew. Each Tuesday he'd spend the whole morning looking at his watch.

'Well, I'd best be going to meet Cyril,' he'd say. 'I'll just have a do with my rotovator.'

Her face stiffened: D'Radcliffe savings stamps are not transferable. I'm leaving. I'm going to Canada. She nodded: of course, whenever he noticed anything was missing, I told him:

'Well, maybe someone picks your pocket when you're out drinking?' I said.

Mrs Coop turned off the tap. After that, she looked at the back door: that draught from Fee's flap chills you right to the bone. She shook her head:

'On the *right*,' I said. 'Put it on the *right*.'

She swallowed as she felt the draught: but he put it on the left. She licked her lips again, then looked down at her feet: he bought me those yellow sheep skin slippers to make up for it. She frowned: I still felt that draught though. I told him so:

'I can still feel that draught,' I said.

She flexed her toes: these are better from *Damart* in burgundy.

As she returned to the pressure cooker, her stomach rumbled: he always says that about the smell of gammon:

'The smell of gammon could wake the dead,' he says.

With a wooden spoon, she stirred the contents: *glop*, he'd call this.

'Well, it might be glop, but at least it's tasty,' she said. Then sniffing, she glanced inside: no. She wiped the corner of her mouth, then twisted the lid onto the pressure cooker: it seems like yesterday.

Mrs Coop flexed her toes: these are better: from *Damart* in burgundy: £12.99 plus a free set of coasters. She flexed her toes again, then moved to stand in front of the Marmite: the pattern on the coasters was hand painted tea cups. She shook her head as she picked up the plate of buttered toast and Marmite: I would have preferred real tea cups, *not* coasters. Biting her lower lip, she stared at her feet: maybe I'll ring *Damart* and ask about thicker tights; trousers are out of the question.

When Mrs Coop reached the refrigerator door, she stopped. She held the plate in one hand, then pushed the door shut.

'Well, I can't fix the slant on the house,' he says.

She waited, but the door didn't swing open again.

Watching the linoleum, Mrs Coop moved forward, then stopped when the linoleum butted up against the carpet. Looking up, she felt for the switch, and when she pressed it, the hallway lighted, shaded pink. She waited until the fluorescent light flickered off behind her; then she stepped out of the kitchen onto the carpet, and in the darkness behind her, the tap continued to drip, scattering droplets of cold water over the grease in the tin tray at the bottom of the sink.

She eyed the telephone: there's no point ringing, not at this time of day, I mean, *night*.

Eight

Mrs Coop hid it in the bottom of her handbag: Dorothy won't know; she won't look this far. She listened: it's that motorcycle next door but two: he should start it quietly. She inspected the shine on her best shoes, then positioned her handbag in the middle of the largest cushion on the sofa.

'Good morning!' she said, and sucking butter from beneath her thumbnail, she approached the wall. 'You're smiling,' she said, and she felt inside the sleeve of her best dress and removed a handkerchief. Then she dusted the photograph of her husband. 'It's better when you smile,' she said.

Looking over her shoulder, she regarded the bare chimney breast: after Aunt Aggie died, we used to keep Malcolm's photograph there, but he was always fussing over it.

'I'm telling you it's not central,' he'd say, so we hung it behind him.

Then he didn't like it there either.

'I feel like someone's watching over my shoulder all the time,' he'd say.

Mrs Coop nodded: but now he doesn't bother.

She glanced at the sofa, then scrutinised the photograph next to the armchair: of course, Malcolm still thinks he's every bit as fetching as he was when he made Lance Corporal.

She smudged the glass as she stroked over his hair, then tweaked at the two shadows on his cheeks: well, he's not lost so much on top, but there's no sign of dimples anymore when he smiles. You can't see anything for wrinkles, these days when he smiles. She stepped away from the photograph: of course, he doesn't smile much these days, but he *used* to! Mrs Coop grinned, then covered her mouth.

'At least when I smile I haven't lost my teeth,' he says, and then he makes that gummy face at me.

She pursed her lips at the photograph, then looked at her wrist: when I showed Malcolm the crack, he said it was seven year's bad luck, and I told him:

'Well, it isn't a mirror; it's a watch face.'

Wiping her mouth, she regarded her handbag, then moved to stand in front of the television by the bay window and parting the curtains, she looked out:

'So how's Fee this morning?' she said.

She scowled at the turquoise paint: it's Malcolm's car, not Fee's rose, that blocks the light. She dropped the curtains, then looked down at the digital clock on the video: I don't trust that; you can't tell if it's three, six, or eight with the lights burned out. She looked at her wrist: Dorothy always comes by eleven. She turns up for her elevenses like clockwork. I could set my watch if it wasn't still in the shop.

'We'll just have time for some toast before we go,' she says.

Mrs Coop rubbed the ingrown hair on her chin, then felt for the drawstring on the curtains: well, that's all Dorothy does when she comes round: I bet she never eats at hers. After opening the curtains, she swallowed: besides: I don't *like* toast. A bit of plain bread does me just fine, with some butter. I tell Malcolm his Marmite just spoils the butter.

Her good eye widened: not the new milkman? She grinned: no, it's Pat. She waved as the postman stepped over the low wall that separated her front garden from Mrs Bamber's: no, he's not stopping. She waved again, then tapped on the window.

'Good morning!' she answered, and she watched him stumble as he neared the other wall: it's that brick Malcolm put there to stop him crossing over. He's always moving it about.

She blinked twice: well, *I* do now; Malcolm would want it kept going.

She opened her mouth again: I must ring *Damart* about my tights. I bet the Queen doesn't wait. I bet she doesn't wait an *hour*: I won't be a minute, they say when *she* rings up. I bet she doesn't have to *ring* at all.

Gripping the curtains to steady herself, Mrs Coop regarded the clock on the video: whatever it is, I've still plenty of time before Dorothy arrives. With one hand, she reached for the cornet on the wall behind the television: of course, I used to keep my savings stamps in here, but then one day I had trouble getting them out. She rubbed the scratch and then the dent in the brass, and after that, she felt inside.

'This could do with a polish,' she said, 'only I never have *liked* polishing.' Puffing out her cheeks, Mrs Coop held the instrument to her lips, then waited. 'I never could do that,' she said, and she lowered the instrument, 'not since I was little. I've no lungs for it.'

She hung the cornet back on the wall: of course, if Popsy had known, about that scratch, he'd have leathered me twice as hard. She pressed her thumb over the end of the mouthpiece: to this day

I swear it wasn't me who dented it. I swear to this day.

'Sugar!' she said as she stubbed her thumbnail against the wallpaper, then turned the cornet over: when Popsy saw the dent, he made me take his belt off.

'One thing you must never do is touch my cornet,' he said.

She sucked her thumb: after he finished, he made me sit on the floor and listen while he played the winning tune. That old linoleum was freezing against my bum, and Popsy was right: it didn't sound anything as good as it did for his competition. What was its name? She glanced at her handbag: of course, he loved playing in that brass band for awhile.

'It's practice makes perfect,' he said, 'practice, practice, *practice.*'

She puffed out her cheeks: when his band won, they had a free train ride down to London for the concert. It was the best of the brass bands, and when he got back, he gave me his postcard of Buckingham Palace. Then he told us about London.

'The beer's flat, and it costs an arm and two legs,' he said.

'So you were *legless*,' Aunt Aggie said.

Mrs Coop puffed her cheeks out as she moved to stand in front of the fire: of course, for days after, Aunt Aggie would only speak to me:

'It's because I didn't buy her the crown jewels,' Popsy said.

Well, Aunt Aggie told me years later:

'It's a brothel he'd been to in London. There were six of them went after that concert. Everyone's talking; it's up and down the street.'

Licking her lips, Mrs Coop stared at the display cabinet in the alcove: it looks like mahogany. Swallowing, she stepped towards it, then felt along the back for the light switch.

'There,' she said as the florescent light flickered inside the cabinet: I like the mirror at the back; it's *doubling.*

Comparing both totem poles, Mrs Coop frowned: Polly's totem pole's fallen over. She stepped closer: her red Indians too. She removed her husband's glasses, then regarded the plastic dolls toppled in a heap inside the cabinet: the Knott Street tribe, Malcolm calls them. There must be nearly two dozen, not including their babies. It's the only thing Malcolm doesn't try to rearrange into rows. She tapped the glass: that was always Polly's trouble: she never knew when enough was enough.

Mrs Coop pressed against her stomach, then looked at her wrist: she was always getting me eggs and sausages when she worked on that farm. When Freddy Mampy couldn't get anything special in for Christmas, Polly blamed the P.O.W. farm labourers for stealing.

'That's why they're shortages,' she said, and she explained how farmers down South were complaining. Then she told the story about the one who was fined for giving his P.O.W.'s rat poison in their rations. Mrs Coop peered at the clock on the video: Freddy said he didn't think P.O.W.'s should have any rations.

She blushed: of course, Polly never could just *give* anything either; she'd always hide it for me to find when I was least expecting. She scratched her leg: that time I'm in the privy, and I reach for the bum papers; I feel them, and wrapped up inside are three sausages! She squeezed her thigh: well, *anyone* could have found them.

After Mrs Coop inspected her wrist, she touched her eye patch: Polly really went over the top when it came to surprises. Watching out the window, her good eye twitched: I'll never forget that time when Aunt Aggie was on the mend from her chesty pains, and Polly turns up on the doorstep, completely unexpected: she said she was going back home for Christmas. Then next thing, it's Christmas

Eve, and Polly's there on our doorstep, dressed up like Santa Claus.

'Guess what I have in my sack!' she says.

Mrs Coop rubbed her chin: it was a Siamese twin goose, and there was one head, but *two* bodies.

'It's a goose on one side, and a *gander* on the other,' Polly said, and she advised Aunt Aggie to wipe the goose grease on her chest with some onions.

Then after we'd eaten, she made something up with the goose grease, but Aunt Aggie wouldn't use it. Truth is Aunt Aggie was the one who liked to do the remedies. She was forever doing up a knitbone paste for my ankle. I'd tell her it was mended:

'Well, this'll *keep* it mended,' she'd say.

Of course, it was murder trying to keep that smell of grease inside the house. Dorothy would have been onto us straight away, but the Resnicks never said a word about it and neither did the Jepsons, no, the Knowles. *They* never said a word.

Mrs Coop looked at her wrist, then turned to read the clock on the video: I can't see it from here. She walked back to the television: when Dorothy comes, I'll tell her I've already had my bread and butter; that'll stump her. When she spreads her marmalade out, it's as thick as her toast. I always say so under my breath:

'Marmalade doesn't grow on trees, you know.'

Sucking on her thumbnail, Mrs Coop moved away from the television, and with her back to the fire, she stared at her handbag: of course, Dorothy never takes the hint. She probably can't hear it for chewing.

Sniffing, she turned, then frowned at the row of Christmas cards on the mantel: he's always doing that; he's always putting everything in rows.

'Malcolm, they're Christmas cards, not carrots,' I said.

Reaching out, she selected the centre card: it's nice of George to keep in touch. I've never had a velvet Christmas card before. She opened the card: George says reindeers really do have velvet on their antlers. After shutting the card, Mrs Coop stroked the velvet: of course, the sleigh's the same, and so is Santa's beard. With her thumb, she compared the texture of velvets: I remember when velvet first came out with that New Look from Paris: the mayor's wife had a collar on her best dress made from it, only it was from *local* velvet.

Mrs Coop tapped the card:

'And now velvet's on Christmas cards. Things *are* getting better,' she said.

She returned the card to the mantel, then stepped away from the fire towards the display cabinet: I'll never forget that Christmas Eve when Polly turned up on our doorstep with George. Typical of Polly: she'd given us no warning. All she said when she hugged me was,

'We thought we'd surprise you for Christmas!'

She said it in an American…no, in a *Canadian* accent.

Mrs Coop pinched her lower lip: talking like that about the flight over, she didn't seem like the same Polly. She was *bigger* than I remembered:

'Are you sure you're the Polly Smith who worked on the Cuckoo Brothers' farm during the War?'

Well, she was: first she explained to George why they were called the Cuckoo Brothers, and then she told the story about the Siamese twin goose, and it was only at the end that she let on it wasn't Siamese at all: instead it was two geese she'd stitched together.

'I should have done it the other way round,' she said.

Mrs Coop held up two fingers: of course, Malcolm always told Aunt Aggie and I it wasn't a Siamese twin goose, but we never believed him. Well, he wasn't there to see it.

She flared her nose at the photograph next to the armchair: of course, Malcolm's always one for spoiling stories. She looked back at the lowest shelf in the display cabinet: when Aunt Aggie went to work for that widower who'd been out to live in Africa, she told us he had so many shirts, she had to put six on a hanger, one over the other, when she'd finished with his ironing.

'Now isn't that rich?' she said.

Malcolm pounced at that:

'Why can't he afford more hangers if he's so rich?' he said.

He didn't realise Aunt Aggie was just fishing.

Grinning, Mrs Coop regarded the top two shelves of the display cabinet: they're like dominoes when they go over. She held up six fingers: of course, I couldn't get over the sound of Polly's voice. Then George came back in with all those presents, and I said that some things never changed.

'Polly never knew when enough was enough,' I said; then I told that story about the sausages and the bum paper.

Mrs Coop held up three fingers: she sounded different, but it was definitely the same Polly: after we'd unwrapped the maple leaf t-shirts and the maple leaf teacups, Polly gave us the scrap book of pressed maple leaves, and Malcolm told her:

'We have so many maple leaves now, we could make our *own* forest.'

It was next to the first thing he said all night; he was very quiet.

Mrs Coop looked over her shoulder: he was very quiet, which was unusual.

Turning back to the display cabinet, she frowned at the heap of plastic Indian dolls: that's when I realised there wasn't a single one of Polly's other presents in sight, so when the Indians started arriving, I set them up in the display cabinet. She bit her lower lip: of course, Aunt Aggie wouldn't like them hobnobbing with her silver tea set. She'd turn in her grave at that. Mrs Coop shook her head, then eyed her husband's photograph.

'Well, she would if she hadn't been cremated!' she said.

She scrutinised the display cabinet: I'll just check again for chance I dreamed it. I always worried he'd find them. With both hands, Mrs Coop reached for the cushion on the armchair; then holding it out level in front of her, she let go of the tassels and frowned when she saw where it landed: it always bounces, no matter how I hold it. With the toe of her slipper, she positioned the cushion; then with one hand, she gripped the armchair and kneeled: Malcolm didn't like it when that widower gave Aunt Aggie the miniature silver tea set; he said the widower was just trying it on.

'He's over eighty,' said Aunt Aggie. 'The only thing he's trying on are his shirts!'

Mrs Coop grasped the cabinet with both hands and rolled it forward. Then she stopped to look over her shoulder at the door to the front room: at least I remembered to close it. She listened: no matter how I do it, something always rattles; Malcolm might hear it one day. She moved backwards on her knees, then placed the cushion to the right before she twisted the cabinet sideways out of the corner. As she repositioned the cushion, she hiccuped, then knelt on it again, and with her good eye closed, she took a deep breath while she lifted the corner of the carpet.

'Eleven…three…*one*,' she said, and she opened her good eye and rolled the carpet back to the crease. Then she let go and stared at the lining beneath the carpet: no wood lice, no spiders.

'Aunt Aggie always said odd numbers are lucky,' said Mrs Coop, and she clasped the torn corner of the lining, then closed her eye and counted:

'Three…one…eleven,' she said, and she peered into the hole in the floorboards: no wood lice, no spiders in here either. She hiccuped, then took a deep breath and felt inside the space: no savings stamps either. Maybe it *wasn't* a dream? Mrs Coop let go of the carpet, then rolled it back into the corner of the room: some squirrel I'd make.

She puffed out her cheeks:

'I'd *starve* if I'd been born a squirrel,' she said.

She puffed her cheeks again, then sighed: now where would I have put them? Hiccuping, she rolled the display cabinet back into the corner, and holding her breath, she waited. Then with both hands, she gripped the armchair: one day I won't get back up; then what'll I tell him? Releasing her breath, she lifted herself up right.

'I'll tell him I was polishing Aunt Aggie's silver,' she said, and she strained to straighten her back. 'I'll need to have the polish with me though,' she added, and she hiccuped. 'No, I'll tell him I've just forgotten it.' She glanced out the window, then winced at the sound of her ankle cracking when she stepped away from the armchair.

'Now that's done it,' she said, and hiccuping, she took three steps forward and landed on the sofa. 'Thank goodness for all these cushions. You can't have too many cushions,' she said, and she prodded several of the cushions before she placed the largest one on her lap.

Noticing her toppled handbag, she held her breath while she stroked the repaired embroidery on the cushion: it's a sign of wind. I told Malcolm that as soon as we saw the feathers. Then those gales arrived, so Fee *did* warn us when she tore Polly's cushion. Mrs Coop scratched her thumbnail on the stitching: if I'd have listened to Fee rather than Malcolm, we could have covered over Aunt Aggie's plot. There's that old tarpaulin beneath the stairs.

When a shadow darkened the room, Mrs Coop looked out the window:

'Dorothy?' she said, and she put the cushion on top of her handbag, then crossed her legs and straightened her dress before she regarded her husband's armchair: he's made a shape in his chair; you can almost see him slouching.

'Malcolm, don't slouch,' she said. 'It'll give you indigestion,' she added, and she blinked slowly: that doily on the back needs washing. It's that compost coming off his hair. 'It's *soiling*!' she said.

She stared at the slouching shape her husband had made in the armchair: I'll never forget that Sunday after we first met: he showed me the greenhouses behind Grand Venture Park. First he showed me all those pots of things he and the other lads were growing. I'm in my best dress. I'm smiling and asking questions, but all I'm thinking is how hot it is inside. I'm thinking it's hot enough to bake bread inside, and he's telling me what each pot is officially, and then what it is to the rest of us, and it's so hot, I can even feel the heat coming off *him*. Then suddenly he sees:

'You're sweating! Wipe your face!' he says, and he gives me his handkerchief.

Mrs Coop blushed.

'That lace doily needs washing again. It's the compost coming off your hair,' she said, and she made a sour face at the armchair. Then she wiped her forehead: after that, he showed me the different types of dirt they used, and he picked up a handful of his favourite, and he told me about the different types of manure that went into it and how much each manure cost by the ton.

'They *buy* that?' I said. 'The Council buys that by the *ton*?'

Mrs Coop blinked: I'd never sweated so much in all my life. She blinked again, then lifted the cushion.

'Not even with the *change*,' she said, and she undid the clasp and felt inside her handbag.

Then at the sound of the diesel engine rumbling outside, she snorted.

'Dorothy?' she said.

She sniffed: I don't smell toast.

Mrs Coop closed her handbag, then tapped on the repair to the cushion as she peered at the display cabinet: I can't remember if I stood them up again or not. If Dorothy sees, she might start poking about. She stared at the display cabinet, then put on her glasses and tilted her head.

'Yes,' she said. 'there's that white top on the totem pole.'

She touched her hair: Polly explained:

'It's a bald eagle,' she said.

'It's got feathers, though, not like a vulture,' George said.

Mrs Coop removed her glasses: of course, when we first met George, we were speechless.

'This is George,' said Polly, and it turns out George is short for *Georgina*.

Mrs Coop gripped her handbag: here's me sending handkerchiefs and ties all those years. She dabbed at the corner of her good eye: they never said anything about that, though, and George still keeps in touch. She sends us a Christmas card each year: *religiously*.

Mrs Coop nodded at the mantelpiece; then she stared at the empty armchair: I kept my savings stamps there for awhile after I saw that spy film with Sir Anthony what's his face. Right under Malcolm's nose, they were. She hiccuped: well, bottom. She hiccuped again; then took a deep breath and held it: I used to keep them there until that time he got uncomfortable and started prodding the cushion.

Her face went red as she watched Mrs Bamber step over the wall separating their front gardens: she's getting too familiar; she never used to do that. Hiccuping, she waved back at Mrs Bamber, then listened for the bell: I don't hear it.

She hiccuped.

'Elsie, have you got your handbag?' asked Mrs Bamber as she stepped into the room. 'The taxi's outside waiting,' she said, and she indicated Mrs Coop's coat.

Swallowing, Mrs Coop looked at her wrist:

'I've already had my elevenses, she said, and she hiccuped. 'There's no marmalade,' she added, ' for your toast,' she hiccuped, and feeling beneath the cushion, she gripped her handbag as Mrs Bamber took her by the elbow: Dorothy's always asking after my handbag. She wants me to pay for the taxi.

110 ∎

Nine

When they reached the end of the ward, Mrs Coop did not reply. She waited at the foot of the bed until Mrs Bamber's back was turned; then she felt between the bed railings.

'He's definitely getting his colour back,' repeated Mrs Bamber. She set the stack of magazines on the bedside cabinet, then placed Mrs Coop's handbag on top. 'His cheeks are going rosy,' she said, and after inspecting the man sleeping in the next bed, she began to draw the curtain between them. 'Don't you notice how Malcolm's cheeks are going rosy?' she said, and when she had drawn the curtain around the end of his bed, she repeated her question, then joined Mrs Coop.

Without answering, Mrs Coop squeezed her husband's toes, then moved to the side of the bed. She shaded her face with one hand, then prodded her husband's ribs with the other.

'He's definitely getting smaller,' she said, and she stepped backwards as Mrs Bamber moved behind her towards the window.

'His roses smell nice!' said Mrs Bamber. She manoeuvred around Mrs Coop, then sniffed the spray of roses in the vase on the windowsill. Bending closer, she sniffed again, then held her hand over the radiator. 'It's a nice view from up here,' she said. 'You can see inside the new grounds.' She stood on her tiptoes. 'That nurse with the club foot said you could watch a match from up here if you wanted.'

Mrs Coop regarded the drips hanging from the stand on the other side of the bed.

'He's getting smaller,' she said. 'He's definitely getting smaller.'

Watching the heart monitor, Mrs Bamber approached the bed.

'He's just lost a bit of weight, that's all,' she said, and she listened to his breathing.

Mrs Coop stepped closer. She reached through the bed railings and felt for her husband's hand. When she gripped it, she lifted his thumb.

'No, he's smaller,' she said, and she measured her thumb against his.

'He's just lost some weight,' said Mrs Bamber. She pressed on the back of the armchair, rolling it nearer to the bed, then tugged gently on Mrs Coop's sleeve. 'Give us your coat,' she said, and she tugged again.

'Thumbs don't lose weight,' said Mrs Coop, and she made her arms rigid as she inspected her husband's face. Then she dropped her arms to her side and stared at the linoleum while Mrs Bamber unfastened the buttons on her overcoat.

'Oh, you don't know, it's surprising,' said Mrs Bamber. 'My mother's fingers are like twigs. You could *snap* them,' she said, and she glanced at Mrs Coop's husband, then cleared her throat. 'You can smell Malcolm's roses from the other end of the ward,' she said.

Mrs Coop looked Mrs Bamber directly in the eyes, and unblinking, she clenched both fists:

'Malcolm always says *my* fingers look like *matchsticks*,' she said as

Mrs Bamber slipped the coat off her shoulders.

'They're nothing like,' said Mrs Bamber, and she folded the coat and hung it over the railing at the foot of the bed.

Still clenching her fists, Mrs Coop stared at the clouds until she felt Mrs Bamber grip her by the elbow.

'Those puffy clouds look like sheep sleeping,' said Mrs Coop, and she pointed.

Rotating an earring, Mrs Bamber assessed the clouds.

'Those *cumulous* clouds, you mean,' she said, and she guided Mrs Coop forward.

'They look like sheep sleeping on the hills,' said Mrs Coop. She watched the clouds as Mrs Bamber helped her to sit in the armchair.

'Yes,' said Mrs Bamber. She hesitated, then touched Mrs Coop's shoulder, and whistling through her nose, she tucked away the frayed strap that was showing.

'*Cumulous*,' said Mrs Coop. 'Malcolm always says that.' She twisted in the chair to look sideways out the window.

'Can you smell his roses all right from where you are?' asked Mrs Bamber.

Mrs Coop flared her nostrils, then coughed.

'No,' she said, 'it smells of Marmite. Where's my handbag?' she asked, and she covered her mouth.

'It's right here,' said Mrs Bamber, and she placed Mrs Coop's handbag in her lap as she moved to the window to pick up the spray of roses. 'I'll just put them here beside you,' she said, and she set them on the bedside cabinet.

'They're not as nice as Fee's,' said Mrs Coop, and she cradled her handbag in both arms, then tapped her foot on the linoleum.

Mrs Bamber hesitated, then looked at her watch:

'Now you'll be all right for half an hour?' she said.

Mrs Coop pursed her lips, then blurted:

'It's an *hour*!' she said.

'I told you I was in a rush today,' said Mrs Bamber. She raised a finger to her lips and spoke in a lowered voice. 'I have to be over at our Petula's for twelve. Remember: Charlie doesn't have play school on a Tuesday.'

Mrs Coop inspected her wrist. She rubbed her forearm, then cradled her handbag before she looked up at Mrs Bamber.

'I'll be glad to have my watch back,' she said.

'Yes, I've not forgotten,' said Mrs Bamber. 'Now you'll be all right, won't you?'

Mrs Coop scratched the flakes of skin on the back of her hand.

'Malcolm's taken it to Dailey and Sons in the Market,' she said, and she cradled her handbag.

'Yes, I won't forget,' said Mrs Bamber. 'Now you'll be all right, won't you? What about the toilet?'

'It's just there,' said Mrs Coop. She pointed to the left, then fumbled to undo the clasp on her handbag.

'It's all right,' said Mrs Bamber. 'You can pay me later. Are you all right for the toilet?'

'Yes, I'll just listen to my cassette tape,' said Mrs Coop, and she felt inside her handbag.

'Remember: we left your cassette at home,' said Mrs Bamber.

'The nurse said you're not to bring it in anymore, remember?' she said.

'Yes,' said Mrs Coop, and she continued to feel inside her handbag. Then her good eye widened, and she withdrew her hand and shut the clasp.

'You can always look through these if you get bored,' said Mrs Bamber, and she tapped the stack of magazines on the bedside cabinet. 'I'll be back in half an hour.'

'*Shh!*' said Mrs Coop, and she pointed at her husband, then watched his heart monitor.

'You'll be right, then?' asked Mrs Bamber.

Mrs Coop cradled her handbag in both arms again and nodded while Mrs Bamber turned to go.

'I'll be off then,' said Mrs Bamber, and after she reached the end of the bed, she waved, then stepped sideways through the gap between the wall and the curtain.

Leaning forward, Mrs Coop inspected the aisle: Dorothy makes a clatter with those shoes; she sounds like horses clomping. Polly's cart horse never made such a noise. She never made such a noise even when she chased that woman down Watersmeeting Road. Well, she wanted to eat the woman's hat. We all agreed it looked just like a fruit bowl.

Mrs Coop scratched the back of her hand.

'Shh!' she said, and she watched her husband, then looked away at the roses on the cabinet: his eyes are sunken; his eyes are sunken in just like Aunt Aggie's. She extended her legs and stared at her best shoes: they're still tight. The girl in the shop said they'd loosen up after I wore them once, but they're still tight, and it's how many times since then? She rubbed the back of her hand: it must be hundreds.

Mrs Coop leaned forward; she inspected the aisle, then whispered:

'Malcolm?' she said. Then she leaned back and fumbled with her handbag, and when she opened it, she stopped and listened. She removed her glasses, then inspected the gap between the floor and the edge of the curtain before she leaned forward again and whispered:

'Malcolm, I brought it like I said I would. See? We're *sharing*,' she said.

She withdrew the parcel from her handbag and placed it in her lap, then gripped it between both legs as she leaned forward to set her handbag on top of the magazines on the cabinet.

Listening, she watched the aisle beneath the curtain: it's raining; it's definitely raining. She looked out the window: no, it's not. It's that drilling on the road below. With one hand, she touched her eye patch. She inspected the aisle again. Then after settling back in the chair, she unrolled her underwear and spread it across her lap. Then she brushed the hairs down on the back of her arm, before she picked up the jar of Marmite and started to unscrew the lid.

When the jar was open, she looked again at the aisle, then studied the gap between the curtain and the wall: it's bigger than a doorway. She set the lid on the bedside cabinet and sniffed: it smells beefy, not yeasty, not *vegetarian*. Holding her breath, she watched her husband: he's definitely getting smaller. She inhaled deeply, then placed the jar of Marmite next to the lid: it's better for him than those roses.

She touched the vase, then slumped back in the armchair, and with the tips of her fingers, she dabbed at the patch on her eye while she watched her husband's profile: he could have blinded me; they said he could have blinded me with those special flowers. She contorted her face: then it'd be me with the glass eye to set on the table.

She tapped her front teeth: just checking. She picked up her underwear, then set it on the cabinet before she gripped each arm of the chair and pressed down: take your time. She concentrated: it's *straining*. She pressed harder, and as the chair rolled backwards, Mrs Coop stood. Then clenching her buttocks, she waited: it's the yeast that does it. Relaxing, she took a deep breath, then eyed the roses: mind the thorns; they're *scratching*.

When she felt the rose petals, she withdrew her hand, and rubbing her fingers, she stared at the Marmite: it's good for you, but he puts it too thick on his toast. She frowned when the drilling started up again: it's good for you; it stops colds, the tar. Smelling it stops colds.

At the sound of footsteps, Mrs Coop covered the Marmite with her underwear, then turned to face the gap between the curtain and the wall: it's bigger than a doorway. She pressed her bladder: I should probably go, now I'm up. Dorothy says not to leave it too late. She looked at her wrist: no, I suppose it can wait. I'll just see, though, for chance it's Dorothy or that nurse. She's forever nattering. She hesitated, then balancing herself with one hand on the bed rails, she shuffled sideways until she stood at the end of the bed. Then she put her foot forward and regarded her ankle: I asked Dorothy to go back for it, but she said there wasn't time.

'I could do with my cane,' she said, and she looked at her wrist, then hobbled towards the edge of the curtain, and when she reached it, she clasped the material in both hands: it's more like plastic, the material; it's more like shower curtains. She sniffed, then peered through the gap down the aisle until the mother disappeared through the swing doors with her two children.

Mrs Coop sneezed as she closed the curtain.

'That's better; it's more private,' she said. She turned, and when she reached the foot of the bed, she gripped the rail and stepped sideways until she reached the bedside cabinet: he's definitely smaller.

As she moved the jar of Marmite, she sniffed the roses: I don't smell a thing. Well, hardly a thing. They're not like Fee's.

'It's freesias Malcolm prefers,' she said. 'What's that?'

She watched the seagulls outside the window: it's bad weather coming. It's blown them inland.

Rubbing her eye patch, Mrs Coop looked at the jar of Marmite: it's wasteful spreading it so thick. I tell him it tastes the same thin as thick. She scrutinised her husband: I tell him it tastes *better* thin than thick. Clamping her mouth shut, she regarded the roses, then reached for the jar, and breathing deeply, she stuck the tip of her index finger into the Marmite, then stirred a circle: it's like treacle. It's like Aunt Aggie's hair.

She looked at her husband:

'Well, it was before she went grey,' she said, and she sucked on her finger: it's hard to imagine it black; it must be twenty years since Malcolm's hair's been black. She pointed. 'It's that Willacy girl that's caused it; you weren't so grey before she came along,' she said.

Then swallowing, Mrs Coop removed her glasses and read the sign above her husband's bed. Moving her lips, she stepped closer, then frowned: they've misspelled that: it's not one *o*; it's two as in *chicken*. It's two as in *Co-op*.

She considered the curtain at the end of the bed.

'I'll tell Dorothy to tell the nurse,' she said, and she turned back toward the bedside cabinet. Listening, she hesitated, then dipped her finger into the Marmite before she turned again and stared at her husband. When we had that picnic, I told you:

'Those eyelashes are wasted on a man,' I said.

'Oh, are they?' you said.

She touched her husband's lips, then slipped her finger inside his mouth: it was the first time I'd tasted strawberries. He grew them himself. She pressed up, then down against his teeth.

'Go on,' she said, 'there's no toast, and there's no butter.' She pressed down again. 'Go, on: open up,' she said. She shook her head, then rubbed the Marmite across her husband's teeth as she watched his eyelashes: come to bed eyelashes. Polly was right about that.

After several moments, she withdrew her hand, then pinched closed his lips and as she felt for the lid next to the Marmite, her stomach rumbled: it's him stopping here at nights that gives me indigestion. She screwed the lid onto the jar, and after she opened her handbag, she put the Marmite inside and closed the clasp. Then she turned to look at her husband.

'It gives me indigestion,' she said, and she approached the bed, then wiped his lips with the back of her hand, and when she finished, she whispered. 'Malcolm,' she said, 'if you tell me where you've hidden my savings stamps, I'll redeem them. I'll never mention that Willacy girl again,' she added.

She waited, then cleaned her hand on the bed sheets.

'They're not transferable,' she said. 'They're in my name; they're worthless to you.'

Gripping the bed rail, Mrs Coop sniffed. She observed her husband's complexion, then turned her head to regard the roses: if Dorothy carries on about his cheeks once more, I'll tell her; I'll shock her with that: I'll ask her if she means his bum cheeks.

She shook the bed: besides, Malcolm doesn't smell of roses. He smells of earth. He smells of earth and smoke. She frowned: except for when he started wearing that perfume for the Willacy girl.

'Imagine a man your age donning about in *perfume*,' she said, and she shook the bed. 'You should be ashamed at that,' she added.

She waited.

'Malcolm, if you tell me where they are, I'll share them,' she said. 'We can go to those silly islands with the sea you're always on about, the ones with the exotic plants in Tescos.'

Staring at the oxygen tube in his nose, she waited. She extended a finger towards it; then she turned and stepped away to sit in the armchair.

When she was settled, she watched her husband's heart monitor: it's like those hills in the Forest of Bowland.

'They should call it the *hills* of Bowland,' she said. 'There were more hills there than *trees*.'

She frowned at the heart monitor: of course, he'd prefer a television. I bet he misses his sport. I bet he misses his radio. She clapped her hands: Malcolm likes his cheering. Her good eye widened as she reached for a tissue: he's *dribbling*.

Ten

She inspected her watch: it's been hours. It's been hours since they brought Malcolm's meal. She tapped the watch face: I've warmed it twice; I swear he makes a point of being late.

With the back of a fork, she scraped the meal into the carrier bag lining the bin beneath the kitchen sink: he's got to eat something soon; he must be starving without his new potatoes. Well, without any potatoes. She stroked her chin: when we used to leave ginger snaps out for Father Christmas, they were always gone in the morning. Malcolm's hollow leg will be empty these days.

She set the tin tray in the sink.

'It's not like Malcolm wasting his meals,' she said.

Humming, Mrs Coop removed the carrier bag from inside the bin. She shut the door, then stared at the frosted glass before she switched on the outside light. Then she looked down at the cat flap: that was the start of it.

'Well, if that Willacy girl wasn't poisoning Fee, what was she doing at the back door that time of night?' I said.

I told the vet, but Malcolm interrupted.

Mrs Coop opened the back door and stepped outside: well, I didn't know then, did I?

'Now there's a draught! It's enough to take your breath away!' she said, and with one hand she covered her mouth and waited: that old stone wall used to block the light to his cold frame. She smirked: whenever he propped open the lid, Fee was straight inside of it. She liked to lie on top of what he was growing and do her business on the seed trays.

Mrs Coop listened, then looked at the sky: they never stop, those aeroplanes. At least their lights are cheerful at night. Of course, they're too fast for me to see these days, flashing.

Clutching the carrier bag in both hands, Mrs Coop stepped forward until she reached the cracked paving slab: I know what I forgot; I forgot my *cane*. Rubbing her eye patch, she looked over her shoulder.

'I forgot to shut the kitchen door as well,' she said, and she covered her mouth and waited as she watched the back of Mrs Bamber's house: there's no lights on. She looked at the back of the rented house next door: just that one in the bathroom, but they won't bother if they see me: we hardly speak.

She watched Mrs Bamber's upstairs window: that doesn't mean there's no one home. I remember after the bombing when the Cuckoo Brothers turned Polly and the other girls in for showing light through their windows. When they interviewed Polly, she told them about the Cuckoo Brothers:

'They're peeping Toms. That's the call they make if there's something to see. They're not even bothered about the seasons,' she said.

Of course, Polly quit working there after.

'It was the Cuckoo Brothers who should have been fined for *peeping*!' she said.

Mrs Coop stepped around the cracked paving stone. She

paused, then continued until she reached the privy at the bottom of the yard. When she heard the motorcycle, she waited: I should have put my coat on first. It's goose pimpling, this weather.

Shading her eyes from the outside light, she looked over her shoulder at the door: it's open. I forgot the key. She headed towards the house: Malcolm says vandals steal anything these days.

'They'll steal the shoes right off your feet,' he said, and he read it from his newspaper.

When she reached the back door, she wiped her feet on the mat inside the kitchen.

'They'll steal your *trainers*,' she said, and she grinned at her slippers, then frowned: no, it's a carrot. It's a *slice* of carrot! She inspected the carrier bag: it's dripping. They always have holes in them these days. They're only plastic.

Holding the carrier away from her, she crossed the kitchen to open the bread bin, then felt inside with one hand. She hesitated: no, I'll need two. After wiping her nose, she set the carrier bag on the cutting board: I'll have dripped a trail of it across the back yard. Popsy's pigeons would make a meal of it. She grinned: then they'd make their *own* trail; Aunt Aggie hated that.

Mrs Coop prodded the bread, then placed it on the cutting board next to the carrier.

'I told Dorothy I don't like it kept in plastic; I told her I don't like it ready sliced,' she said.

Inhaling, she looked inside the bread bin, then inspected it with both hands: he should think of a better place to hide the key.

'Well, what if they break in and decide to make a sandwich? *Then* they'll find the key,' I said.

She raised an eyebrow.

'Well, they do if they're on *drugs*,' she said. 'They don't think about *time* if they're on *drugs*.'

After withdrawing both hands, Mrs Coop, wiped her fingers on the front of her cardigan, then fumbled for the chain around her neck, and looking over the rims of her glasses, she peered into the bread bin: no, it's not here. She pushed her glasses up from the tip of her nose: I told Malcolm his head was too wide.

'Your head's *twice* the width of mine!' I said, but he insisted I wear them.

She wiped crumbs off the front of the lenses, then removed the glasses: I must've unlocked it already; I'm not used to the privy being padlocked. It's with his aerial being broken, and it wasn't even here: it was in *town*. She shut the bread bin; then she opened it and put the loaf back inside.

'I'll just get Aunt Aggie's coat,' she said, and turning, she headed for the refrigerator. Then before she stepped onto the carpet in the hallway, she wiped her feet on the linoleum and adjusted the magnetic maple leaf.

'The carpet's better on your feet,' she said as she watched the carrot on her slipper: first I thought it was part of the *bouquet*! It's the unfastening that gets me with the Velcro. When she reached the curtain beneath the staircase, she hesitated: don't think about it. Aunt Aggie would say so:

'It's all water under the bridge,' said Mrs Coop, and she opened the curtain, then reached inside for the coat. 'It's all water under the bridge,' she said as she put the coat on, then tied the belt around her waist: Malcolm thought it was its tail at first.

'No, that's a tassel!' Aunt Aggie said.

She glanced at the telephone, then looked at the door to the back room. She shook her head, then took several steps forward, and when she stepped onto the linoleum, she shaded her good eye from the florescent light as she advanced towards the carrier bag: it's the mint sauce that's put him off; Malcolm doesn't like mint sauce. He doesn't like any sauce: *yakum*, he calls it.

She pursed her lips: he says it like he's being sick.

'*Yakum*!' she said.

There's no need for it.

Holding the carrier bag, Mrs Coop stepped forward, and with each step, she watched the linoleum until she reached the back door: it's dripping; I'll need a mop after.

'I forgot to close that,' she said as she stepped outside, then closed the door. Malcolm says I'm always leaving things. She took two steps, then stopped.

'I forgot my cane again,' she said, and she covered her mouth as she looked towards the fence: no, Dorothy might hear. She's always listening out for me:

'You were very quiet in the night,' she says. 'I listened, but I didn't hear a peep from your side.'

'*Peep*!' said Mrs Coop, and she covered her mouth.

She waited, then stepping forward again, she scrutinised the ground: where is it? I can't see it for my shadow. She stopped, then moved sideways to avoid the cracked paving slab, and following her shadow, she stopped at the privy door: no, I took that padlock off, didn't I? She stared at the latch: I wonder what I did with it? I wonder what I did with that key?

She felt inside her coat pockets: no, the wrong ones. It's too many pockets, I have. She slipped the carrier bag over one wrist and undid the belt on her coat; then she felt in her cardigan for the penlight: my toilet torch, I call it. I can't stand that fan whirring, so the whole street can hear it. It whirrs for ages after the light's turned off, but Malcolm says there's no changing it.

'It's *regulation*,' he says.

Mrs Coop pointed the torch at the latch: I know what they'll think. She switched on the penlight, then looked over her shoulder at the back of Mrs Bamber's house, and her good eye widened: if Dorothy sees me, she'll think I'm a burglar; she'll ring that number, and then I'll have to pay.

'Don't dilly-dally,' she whispered, and she pressed down on the latch, then pulled the door towards her, and shining the penlight on the flagstones, she stepped inside, then shut the door.

I forget. I'm forgetting something: it's a spray. She frowned: not *flowers*! After she placed the carrier bag inside the black bin liner, her good eye twitched: I forgot about the spiders. I didn't check first for spiders. I'm like Aunt Aggie.

'Spiders make my skin crawl,' she said, and her face twitched as she pressed the latch on the door.

'I'll just get that spray,' she said.

Then she took a step backwards: no, Dorothy might see. She'll ring that number, and then I'll have to pay. Mrs Coop stepped backwards again, then pointed the penlight at the coil of garden hose hanging in the middle of the door.

'It looks *spidery*!' she said.

She moved the torch to the right and then to the left, and sniffing, she pointed it at the bin liner; then her good eye widened, and she covered her mouth: that time Aunt Aggie and I stopped at Morecambe for Wake's Week, and a batch of them sprang up overnight in the corner of our room. Mrs Coop steadied the light with both hands: they're not bright orange; they're *creamy*, but Aunt

Aggie said so about the orange ones in our room.

'Those are *toadstools*!' she said, and then she said they were deadly. 'They make soars; that's how they *breed*!' she said, and at tea she told the other guests about the woman who was found dead with them growing in her lungs. 'They suffocated her overnight in her sleep,' Aunt Aggie said.

Mrs Coop batted an eyelid: we couldn't believe that landlady with her high prices and her toadstools: when Aunt Aggie told her, she wasn't even bothered.

'Well, there's no other room's free,' she said.

She didn't even offer to remove them, so Aunt Aggie took the chamber pot from beneath the bed and turned it over to cover those toadstools, and we never went back to Morecambe again.

Mrs Coop turned away from the mushrooms, then directed the beam at the zinc bath hanging on the opposite wall: of course, we never used it, not for donkey's years, but I wouldn't let him have it as a water butt after Aunt Aggie died. Mrs Coop scratched her head, then stepped forward and jiggled the bath: each Friday night I went first in front of the fire. I loved it piping hot, the water.

Gasping, she let go of the bath: I felt a web! She took three steps backwards; then, holding her hand in front of her nose, she inhaled: it's that mint sauce. She covered her mouth as she stared at the bath: I remember the fly catcher: *Joe*, he was called, and his top hat was covered in sticking strips; it was crawling in flies. We only came out to see him for that.

'That's *disgusting*,' Aunt Aggie said.

Mrs Coop flared her nostrils: of course, it might be a cobweb. Where do they come from? She curled a lip after she tapped the bath: no, it might bring them out! It's vibrations they feel with their webs.

She took a step backwards: Malcolm was into everything after Aunt Aggie died: he was changing this, changing *that*. She pointed the penlight at the tea chest next to the bath: changing things to suit himself. *Modernising*, he called it. She stared at the garden tools standing on end in the tea chest: *rakes*! She grinned: I'll never forget how Malcolm said so without realising:

'With my job we may not afford a house with a garden, but we'll always have *rakes* of rakes,' he said.

He said it proud.

Mrs Coop wiped the end of her nose, then began to count the rakes: a dolly peg? She stepped forward: it must be Aunt Aggie's. She gripped the handle, and pulling it towards her, she pointed the penlight down into the tea chest.

'No: it's a *spade*,' she said, and she turned to face the stack of egg cartons on the privy seat.

Stepping forward, she pointed her light: that time him behind us up but one invited everyone to see what he'd done. What was his name? He had two brown lumps either side of his nose; Aunt Aggie always said they looked like rabbit droppings.

Mrs Coop shook her head.

'No, I forget,' she said. Looking down, she inspected the stacks of egg cartons. When he showed us what he'd done, he seemed right proud, like he owned two cars, and after he asked us, Aunt Aggie gave me a clout round the ears.

'Did we want to try it out, *heck*?' I said.

Covering her mouth, Mrs Coop stared at the egg cartons: well, who wants to sit next to someone doing *that*? It's private!

A flush rose in her cheeks: of course, there was that time Mary Clegg and I went with those boys in that one behind where the old

Lower Dunnow Primary School used to be: it wasn't just kissing; it was *worse* what they wanted!

She shivered: of course, it wasn't in use then. She shivered: I'll never forget how Popsy used to bring that oil lamp down with him for heat first thing in the morning. Aunt Aggie would fumble about in the dark:

'It's hours he wastes in there,' she'd say.

Mrs Coop considered the stacks of egg cartons. She moved closer and pointed the penlight; then she shook her head: he's taken the lids off. He's stacked those separately. They're in *rows*: a row of bottoms and a row of tops.

'He's always putting everything in rows!' she said.

She brushed the stacks of egg cartons onto the floor next to the bin liner, then lifted the lid with one hand: he might have put my savings stamps down here; he's definitely oiled the hinges. She sniffed briefly, then pointed the penlight into the space below, and after several moments, she dropped the lid.

'No, I didn't think he'd do *that*,' she said.

As she took a step backwards, her ankle cracked, and teetering, she reached for the spade in the tea chest; then leaning on the handle, Mrs Coop waited: I told him I didn't like the look of the top of that hill:

'What view? You can't even *see* it,' I said.

She leaned more heavily on the spade: it's stabbing. It's stabbing that pain. She blinked: don't go all weepy; I know what Polly could have done with all her Canada maple trees: she could have planted them up in that Forest of Bowland!

Mrs Coop let go of the spade, then limped towards the privy seat, and when she reached it, she turned and inched backwards until she felt the edge against her legs: it's cold, the draught coming off these flagstones, but I'll have to rest; it's stabbing, not aching, my ankle: if I fall, Dorothy will find me.

With one hand on the edge of the seat, she lowered herself, and when she was settled, she pointed the penlight at the floor, then inched the beam across the egg cartons until she located the bin liner: it's ages since I've sat here. It brings back memories: I feel *young*!

Her stomach rumbled.

'*Mad Elaine*, that was the name of Polly's cart horse; she was always running off,' she said.

She reached to her left: they were just here, the bum papers. I told Polly:

'When I saw those sausages wrapped up, you can guess what I thought.'

She did: she said so straight away.

Mrs Coop pointed the penlight at the zinc bath: those were the days when Polly stopped over! Aunt Aggie always said the same thing whenever Polly came round:

'Don't you have a home of your own to go to?' she'd say.

Mrs Coop flexed her toes: the only thing with our privy seat: it cuts off the blood to your feet if you stop too long; it's the edge that's sharp. When Popsy complained, Aunt Aggie always said so:

'*Good*!' she'd say.

Mrs Coop pointed the penlight at her slippers: Popsy always said we could do with a footrest in here. I can hear her now:

'You spend enough time in there as it is. You'll *die* in there.'

Mrs Coop flexed her toes again: well, I better be going; no, I *best* be going. She shined the penlight onto the mushrooms, then covered her mouth: *The Splendide* was the name of that bed and breakfast in Morecambe. Aunt Aggie always called it The Splen*dead* when she told anyone about the toadstools.

'There's no place like home,' Aunt Aggie always said.

Eleven

After Mrs Coop had removed her aunt's zebra skin coat, she returned to the kitchen and stared up at the florescent light: it's flickering: it's like those lights Dorothy had at Petula's wedding, only weaker. Mrs Coop's good eye started to twitch: they don't dance together with steps like *we* used to. Humming, she held out a fork, then took a step forward and two steps sideways: did I know how to Lindy? Well, of course, I did; I wouldn't have been there if I didn't know how to Lindy.

When she bumped into the countertop, she stopped.

'I'm forgetting something,' she said.

She returned to her initial position, and rubbing her hip, she regarded the sink, then placed the fork on top of the empty tray: maybe I can tempt him with his buttered toast and Marmite.

'Malcolm, there's buttered toast and Marmite,' she said as she moved away from the sink, and when she reached the cutting board, she picked up the plate. 'I've put it on thick,' she said.

On her way out of the kitchen, she paused in front of the refrigerator door: it's a goose on one side and a gander on the other.

Humming, she stepped onto the carpet in the hallway, and when she entered the back room, she stopped suddenly: it smells of smoke and earth! She sniffed: it's not supposed to smell like *that*! Rubbing an ache in her side, she sniffed again: the way Polly said it, I'll never forget. It was after the psychic woman's assistant explained about the spirit: Polly nudged me and whispered:

'It'll smell just like *semen*,' she said. 'The spirit will smell just like semen,' and when Malcolm asked what she was saying, Polly batted her eyelids.

Mrs Coop glanced down at her chest, then at the toast, and as she scanned the room, she tilted the plate.

'Malcolm?' she said, and she looked down at the toe of her slipper as several more toast soldiers fell to the floor. 'Malcolm?' she said.

She steadied the plate: of course, Malcolm nearly jumped out of his skin when that spirit asked after Bob Bash: well, Malcolm had only just learned about him that morning!

Her good eye widened as she observed the two soldiers remaining on the plate. Then she looked at the back window: of course, it might be like Popsy feeding his pigeons.

She watched the toast on the floor, then scanned the room again.

She sniffed: that smell's fading, maybe not.

She stepped forward, then stopped suddenly: now that's something.

She examined her slippers: Malcolm's always crunching his crusts.

Sniffing, she headed towards the door, and when she reached it, she held the plate in one hand, and she watched the remaining pair of toast soldiers as she felt for the door handle: of course, two's a bad sign. It's odd numbers that are lucky.

Gripping the door handle, Mrs Coop continued to watch the toast as she inched forward into the hallway: it's smoke and earth. She nodded when the door was closed; then she tilted the plate as she stroked her fingers across the scratches.

'Fee, keep him in there,' she said, and as the toast moved sideways towards the edge, she steadied the plate with both hands, and without taking her eyes off the two soldiers, she stepped to the telephone table beneath the staircase: of course, he might be *sharing* with two. That would be one each that he left on the plate.

'*That's* lucky,' she said.

She pursed her lips: but I prefer bread and butter.

Mrs Coop grinned, then frowned when she saw the cassette player next to the telephone: I wish it hadn't broken; I miss the rhyme they do at the end of it. With one hand, she pushed the cassette player out of the way: better. Then as she set down the plate, her ankle cracked:

'Turnips!' she said, and she covered her mouth.

Listening, she waited.

Then with both hands, she gripped the edge of the table, and leaning to her right, she stared at the telephone and counted: it's never good when my ankle cracks. She lifted a hand and wiped her eye with her index finger: don't go weepy on me. After she dried her hand on her cardigan, she put on her glasses.

'Thirteen, nine, seven, nine,' she whispered, and she lifted the receiver; then pressed two buttons. As she pressed them again she spoke loudly. 'Nine, nine' she repeated. Then looking at her cassette player, she shook her head. 'No: Dorothy said I would have to pay if Malcolm wasn't here. It's best not to ring.' She hung up, then considered the remaining toast soldiers before she looked at the door to the back room.

'Malcolm,' she said, 'if you tell me where my savings stamps are, I'll share them. We'll go to those islands with the special trees that grow outside. We won't have to fly.'

After tracing a finger along the deepest crease in her palm, Mrs Coop picked up the plate.

'There's more buttered toast and Marmite,' she said. 'The toast is burned!' She grinned. 'There's sport on the television too. There's cheering!' she said, and she picked up the plate and stepped towards the front room.

'Malcolm!' she called.

She set the plate next to the candle stub on top of the television; then she lit the candle and cupped her hands over the flame: it's not like that psychic woman's candelabra, but it'll do. It'll *have* to. Sneezing, Mrs Coop raised her hands away from the flame: Polly kissed me when I gave her the psychic woman's candelabra.

'I'll never forget you,' she said.

Then she kissed me again, on the other cheek, and she kept saying it. 'I'll never forget you,' she said.

Polly was going to Canada:

'There's wide open spaces, and no one knows you, she said. 'Everything's bigger; the *sky's* bigger,' she said.

Well, it would have suited Polly: she was very tall.

Mrs Coop's good eye widened: I hope Malcolm can't hear me thinking! Sparks would fly!

'Malcolm,' she said, 'there's sport on the television, and there's buttered toast and Marmite: it's *thick*!'

She blew on her hands, then stepped backwards to look at the clock on the video: Malcolm always has his toast and Marmite when he comes home. She sniffed: he burns the toast. He makes a point of it to wake me, and when I come down, he's always smoking a cigar.

Mrs Coop frowned: that's what I forgot; it's because I don't like him smoking in the house.

Looking at the television, she stepped forward, and feeling the button, she pressed against the red light: of course, he always leaves the Marmite out if I don't come down. She sniffed, then pressed again: there, *green*! You can hear it first. She watched the screen: and the bread. He leaves the bread out as well. It's gone stale by the morning if I don't come down.

Mrs Coop listened, then slid the lever to the right until it stopped; then she pressed harder against it: no, that's on full. Covering her ears, she stepped away from the television: he'll definitely hear that.

'Malcolm,' she said, 'see: it's sport. There's *cheering*!'

She picked up the plate, and as she walked, she watched the carpet until she stopped in front of the gas fire. Then warming herself, she studied the rag rug: Malcolm can't see the point of this. He says it's enough padding with the carpet. With the toe of her slipper, Mrs Coop nudged a dark speck on the rug: well, it's for sparks: they could burn the carpet. She looked at the gas fire: he says gas fires don't spark, but you never know; all it takes is one.

She watched the television: when we were courting, I asked Malcolm right here on the old sofa:

'Why do they call it football?'

Turning, she stepped forward: and he starts to explain. He slips a finger between the buttons on the front of his shirt, and he starts way back with the history of it.

Watching her slippers, Mrs Coop crossed the room: no wonder

they're always missing if they have to keep kicking that ball between their feet. Well, they can never look up to aim. She stepped sideways to avoid the cushion on the floor: of course, they don't call it kicking: *dribbling*, they call it. When she reached the nest of tables stacked by the door, she looked up at the light switch: I'll never forget when Malcolm first told me.

'Dribbling?' I said, and when I touched that button on his shirt, he raised a hand.

'Shh!' he said, and he turned up the volume on the radio. '*Shh*!' he said, and when his favourite player missed, Malcolm explained. 'He's the best dribbler in the division.'

'*Dribbles*?' I asked when I touched that button again, Malcolm kept a straight face as he explained to me what dribbling was in football.

Well, I wasn't interested.

As Mrs Coop touched the light switch, a spark flashed, and she jerked back her hand. That'll be from the carpet; I'm dragging my feet again. She examined her slippers, then looked sideways at her husband's armchair: or it's him I've upset with the football.

'Sorry, Malcolm,' she said.

She uncrossed her fingers, then wiped them on the handkerchief inside the pocket of her cardigan before she turned off the light switch: well, I'm still not interested. Teetering, she took one step towards her husband's armchair, then waited: it takes some adjusting getting used to this light. I mean *dark*.

She stared at her feet: what we could do with is one of those lights Polly was always writing about:

'There are no switches. You just clap your hands to turn it on and clap them again to turn it off. You never have to leave your seat,' she said.

Of course, by then she'd gone off the wide open spaces, and she was into food and gadgets instead. Malcolm got tired of me reading out her letters:

'In Canada, they always ask: can I get you some *more* steak?'

When Polly visited with George, she said it in her new accent.

'In Canada, they always ask: can I get you some *more* steak?'

Mrs Coop looked at the television: of course, Polly's clapping light would never work in our house, not with all of his cheering.

Watching her feet, Mrs Coop stepped toward her husband's armchair; then as she lowered herself, her stomach rumbled: it seems only yesterday since we went to see that psychic woman.

She crossed her legs, then wiped her mouth as she balanced the plate on her knee: none of us except Polly had ever been to anything like *that* before. We only went along to support that drive for the Spitfire.

Everyone kept saying it:

'What's the old witch going to do? Spit *fire*?'

Mrs Coop looked down at her legs: it was always something back then. We were always raising money for something. She felt for the hem of her dress, then lifted the plate and uncrossed her legs: it's not a bit ladylike the way Malcolm sits. Resting her head on the antimacassar, Mrs Coop set the plate back on her lap: he's sagged the chair. He's sagged the chair into his shape. I told him he would if he always sat in the same position.

She watched the television: it was a shame the police broke it up before Polly could speak to her Gran.

'They hadn't any right to,' Polly said.

When we went dancing after, I kept telling Polly how I wished

I'd gone with her those times she went to see the psychic woman in Blackpool.

'It's all just a hoax,' Malcolm kept saying. 'Why do you think the police broke it up, and why do you think *she* left in such a hurry?' he said.

Then he insisted it was a circus dwarf, not a spirit that came out of the psychic woman's mouth, but Polly put him straight:

'Well, they didn't find that spirit, did they? If it was a circus dwarf, then they would've found him, wouldn't they?'

So Malcolm went on about his trick mirrors:

'That so-called spirit wasn't even in the theatre,' he said.

But Polly wasn't standing down:

'Well, *of course* they used mirrors, but they weren't *trick*,' she said. '*We* were up front, but how could anyone see at the back if they didn't use mirrors? The dwarf was *too small* to see from the back.'

'*Spirit*, you mean,' I said, and Malcolm pounced at that.

Mrs Coop bit into the buttered toast and Marmite: of course, there were no mirrors at the Spitfire raffle they held after, but the candelabra was there. She leaned forward and watched the television: it sounds like something happened. She listened: there's more clapping; there's more cheering.

After several moments, Mrs Coop looked up at the candle: I'm supposed to watch *that*, not the telly. It's Malcolm who watches the telly. She concentrated: when I won the psychic woman's candelabra in the raffle, Malcolm didn't like it. I told him:

'You're afraid of it,' I said, and he told me I must be joking.

Mrs Coop swallowed the toast: he really *was* afraid of it,

though. When I won it that night, the air raid sirens went off just as we were leaving. They hadn't gone off since Malcolm had been on leave, so he thought it was that psychic woman that caused it. He kept saying it over and over inside the shelter:

'I'm telling you: that witch has put the mockers on us,' he said.

After they gave the all clear, the three of us waited. We were the last ones out, and after Malcolm helped Polly up, he took the candelabra and threw it back inside.

'Leave it!' Malcolm said.

But Polly retrieved it: she said we were lucky it landed on those sandbags.

Mrs Coop watched the television: of course, Malcolm had gone by then, so Polly and I had to make our own way home. That's when Polly said what she really thought about Malcolm. We had a row about it.

Mrs Coop stuck out her tongue: Malcolm can think what he likes; that spirit *did* come out of the psychic woman's mouth. When the psychic woman was in her trance, her assistant explained:

'She's drinking spirit water to attract the spirit,' she said.

Mrs Coop removed her husband's handkerchief from the pocket of her cardigan: Mrs O'Riley, was the psychic woman's name. No, she wasn't a psychic: she was a *clairvoyant*.

Mrs Coop grinned: I'll never forget that headline in the paper. Malcolm showed me:

'Ghosts? *O' Riley*, do you expect us to believe that?' the headline said.

Then Malcolm whistled when Polly explained how Mrs O' Riley was really from Glasgow. We didn't get it at first. He said it

142 ■

was like that Scottish comic with the Welsh surname, the one who whistled like a canary: Irvine MacWelsh, he was called. Mrs Coop shook her head: no, his tea kettle did, and he had a canary that whistled like a tea kettle.

Wiping her lips, Mrs Coop watched the television as she chewed the buttered toast and Marmite: it seemed like ages after they'd turned off the lights in the theatre. Malcolm wouldn't give over tickling me. Then the assistant lit the candles one by one until we could see the psychic woman's face all lit up by the candelabra, and we waited while she drank the spirit water.

It was only when her mouth began to froth, just like Polly said it would, that Malcolm stopped tickling me.

Mrs Coop's good eye watered as she spread her husband's handkerchief over the empty plate: it's a bit stiff, this. It's not cold, though. Trying not to swallow, she sucked on her cheeks until saliva welled in her mouth; then she spat.

She waited, then she spat again.

After that, she lifted the handkerchief and held it near her face: no, it doesn't look right. It doesn't look like what that psychic woman spat out. Mrs Coop sniffed: no, it doesn't smell like it either. It smells of Marmite. I always tell Malcolm how Marmite ruins the butter.

She hesitated, then set the handkerchief back on the plate: of course, they might smell *different*. Not all spirits might smell the same. She glanced at the television, then focused on the candle as she moved her lips, and counting down, she watched the television: it's dribbling. They're dribbling all over the place, all over the *field*.

After several moments, she lowered her hand to touch the dab of sputum with the tip of her index finger: it's gone cold. She closed her good eye, then took three deep breaths through her nose before she opened her mouth again and stuck out her tongue: when that spirit emerged from the psychic woman's mouth, Malcolm jumped just the same as I did.

It hovered there in mid-air.

You could see it dripping onto the candelabra: it put the lights out, and when it asked Malcolm if he wanted a word with Bob Bash, Malcolm couldn't speak for trembling. I squeezed his hand, but he couldn't say a word, so I looked at Polly, and she asked after her Gran instead.

'Malcolm,' said Mrs Coop, 'remember when we went to see that psychic woman with Polly after we'd just started courting? Remember when we went to see that Mrs Mc Riley from *Glasgow*?'

Mrs Coop watched the television.

'*Shh!*' she said, and she stuck out her tongue.

She waited: maybe it's my teeth. Maybe they don't leave enough room for the spirit to get out? I'm only small, and that Mrs Riley was huge: she was gi-normous. Nodding, she removed her teeth and placed them in the centre of the handkerchief, then after opening her mouth again, she stuck out her tongue: something's happened; I can *feel* it. Mrs Coop waited; then she closed her mouth suddenly and sat upright with her knees together:

'They've scored!' she said.

She listened, then put in her teeth: I felt it then: I felt a *vibration*.

She sniffed: it smells…it definitely smells familiar.

'Fee?' she said.

She sniffed: it's not a spirit; it's his handkerchief, I'm smelling! She folded the handkerchief, then picked it up and inhaled the scent: after the nurse gave it to me, I put it on his pillow: I'd never been in the house on my own before. She inhaled again: it still smells of him. It's not fading.

She eyed the curtains in the bay window: I can't see Fee's rose. She folded the handkerchief again before she slipped it under the cuff on her cardigan.

'I'm always leaving things,' she said, and she lifted the plate, then set it on the table next to the armchair. 'I forgot to open the curtains, and I forgot that cigar again,' she said. Twisting in the armchair, she spoke to her husband's photograph. 'You're reminding me, like with your television,' she added.

She strained to lift herself out of the chair:

'It's too low,' she said as she stood teetering on the carpet.

Then as she crossed the room, she watched her feet: they shouldn't call them slippers; you could fall over.

Twelve

When she heard the commotion, Mrs Bamber opened the door to the front room.

'Elsie, are you all right?' she asked, and when she saw Mrs Coop, she dropped the bottle of milk and the loaf of bread onto the sofa, then stepped over to the armchair and squeezed Mrs Coop's hand.

'Elsie!' she said. She glanced sideways at the television as she raised a hand, then patted Mrs Coop on the check. 'Elsie, it's me, *Dorothy*, wake up!' she said, and taking care not to touch Mrs Coop with her cosmetic nails, she patted her again on the cheek.

After several rasping breaths, Mrs Coop snorted, then opened her good eye.

'Malcolm?' she said, and her eyelid fluttered as she tried to focus. Then she shut her mouth and rubbed her face. 'Malcolm?' she said.

'No, it's me, *Dorothy*!' said Mrs Bamber.

Mrs Coop tilted her head to the side:

'Malcolm, quit that shouting,' she said.

'It's *Dorothy*!' said Mrs Bamber, and as she took a step backward, she crushed bread into the carpet. 'What?' she said, and leaning forward, she gripped the armchair with one hand as she lifted her foot and removed the bread from the sole of her stiletto.

'Malcolm,' said Mrs Coop, as she felt for her glasses, 'turn it down. It's not cheering; it's *shouting*!'

'No, it's me, *Dorothy*!' said Mrs Bamber, and she dropped the bread onto the plate in Mrs Coop's lap; then after glancing at the pieces remaining on the carpet, she continued to examine her stiletto, then slipped off her shoe.

'Malcolm,' said Mrs Coop, 'Dorothy will think we're rowing.' Mrs Coop put on her glasses and scanned the room, then dabbed at her eye patch as she stared at the television. 'You call that cheering? That's shouting!' she said.

Mrs Coop waited, listening.

'*Hurrah*!' she said. 'Now *that's* cheering.'

Mrs Bamber removed the plate from Mrs Coop's lap.

'Elsie, it's me, Dorothy; you must have been dreaming,' she said, and standing in front of the armchair, she held her shoe upside down by its heal.

'Malcolm, stop shouting,' said Mrs Coop, and she covered both ears. Then she sniffed. 'Malcolm, you're wearing that perfume again,' she said, and she lowered her voice. 'You think I don't notice but I do.' Then as her good eye started to water, Mrs Coop sneezed.

'It's all right, Elsie. It's just the television,' said Mrs Bamber. She glanced over her shoulder, then reaching towards Mrs Coop's lap, she set her shoe on the plate, and after unbuttoning her coat, she stood with one hand on her hip and regarded Mrs Coop's frock. 'You didn't fall asleep down here last night, did you?' she asked.

Mrs Coop looked in her lap.

'Who's…what's *that*?' she said.

'It's me, *Dorothy*,' said Mrs Bamber. She turned on the ball of her foot, then removed the plate from Mrs Coop's lap and set it on top of the display cabinet. 'You didn't fall asleep down here last night, did you?' she asked, and she turned back to face Mrs Coop.

Mrs Coop blinked twice. She opened her mouth, then shut it; then she opened it again:

'Dorothy?' she said, and she looked at the doorway to her right. 'I didn't hear the bell go,' she said, and she looked back at the television, 'not with all that *shouting*,' she added.

'You didn't fall asleep down here last night, did you?' repeated Mrs Bamber

Mrs Coop covered her ears.

'I wish Malcolm would fix that bell. I can't hear it half the time with all of that shouting,' she said, and she watched Mrs Bamber stoop to pick up the Christmas cards that had fallen from the mantel.

'You've put the fire on at least,' said Mrs Bamber. She turned down the gas, then laid the Christmas cards down in the empty space on the mantel, and when she crossed the room to turn off the television, she noticed the candle. 'I thought I smelled something when I came in,' she said. 'You should be careful; I better move it.'

Mrs Coop frowned; she leaned to the side, and lifting her buttock, she prodded the seat cushion.

'Yes, you can take it away. There's nothing but tripe on it anyway,' she said. She examined the palm of her hand, then covered her ears again.

'The taxi'll be here soon,' said Mrs Bamber. 'Have you got your handbag?' Through the bay window, she watched the postman cross the street. Then after she returned to the display cabinet, she set the candle next to the plate and pivoted on her stocking foot to address Mrs Coop. 'Elsie,' she said, as she regarded

Mrs Coop's frock and her slippers, 'you didn't sleep down here last night, did you?'

Mrs Coop licked her lips, then tried to swallow:

'I'm thirsty. Is the kettle on?' she said, and she looked at her watch.

Mrs Bamber regarded the dab of marmalade on Mrs Coop's chin; then she twisted an earring:

'You're wearing the same dress as *yesterday*,' she said.

Mrs Coop wiped her face as she felt the front of her dress:

'It's my best dress!' she said. 'It's a different scarf I'm wearing.' Sucking on the insides of her cheeks, she tasted marmalade, then looked at her watch. 'It's eleven,' she said, and she eyed Mrs Bamber. 'There's marmalade for your toast,' she said, 'but I'll just have bread and butter for mine.'

'We haven't got time; the taxi's on its way,' said Mrs Bamber, and she glanced out the window, then looked beneath the television at the digital clock on the video. 'I told you I didn't have much time today,' she said.

'There's the same time everyday. There's the same time *twice* a day,' said Mrs Coop.

'Are you ready?' asked Mrs Bamber. 'Where's your handbag?'

Mrs Coop pursed her lips, then inspected her watch again:

'Well, what about your elevenses?' she said.

'We can get something at the hospital if you like,' said Mrs Bamber. She looked out the window. 'I'll get your coat and your handbag; I won't be a minute,' she said as she stepped towards the sofa.

Licking her lips, Mrs Coop watched Mrs Bamber limp across

the carpet, then bend to pick up the loaf of bread from the sofa.

'Dorothy,' said Mrs Coop. She tilted her head sideways. 'What's wrong with your ankle?' she asked.

Holding the bread and the bottle of milk, Mrs Bamber looked down at her stocking foot.

'It's just my shoe: I've taken it off,' she said, and she hobbled across the room to the display cabinet.

Mrs Coop advised her:

'*Knitbone* will mend it,' she said.

Mrs Bamber scratched her head:

'It just needs washing. I'll put this milk away and get your coat; I won't be a minute,' she added, and with one hand she lifted the plate off the display cabinet.

After Mrs Bamber had gone, Mrs Coop leaned forward and flexed her ankle: it hurts, but it's not cracking. She looked at the display cabinet, then wiping her chin, she stared at the television:

'Malcolm,' she whispered, 'I'll share them if you tell me where they are.'

She waited.

'We could go on holiday to that island. We wouldn't have to fly.'

She listened, then looked away as the postman stepped in front of the window:

'I must ring *Damart* about those tights,' she said.

Feeling inside the sleeve of her best dress, Mrs Coop removed her handkerchief, and inhaling, she stared out the bay window at the rose bush. 'It's not so big, not for this time of year without its leaves,' she said. She raised her voice. 'Without its flowers,' she added; then she frowned: it's Malcolm's car, not Fee's rose that blocks the light.

She watched out the window, then looked at the television:

'Malcolm,' she whispered, 'they're worthless to you. If you take them to D'Radcliffe's, they'll tell you: my savings stamps are *non*-transferable. They're like Aunt Aggie's bonds: she didn't want you getting your hands on those either.'

'Elsie,' are you ready?' said Mrs Bamber. Shouldering Mrs Coop's handbag, she examined the carpet; then swinging the cane, she crossed the room to wave in the window. 'We better make a move. The taxi's here,' she said, and she approached Mrs Coop. 'Here's your cane,' she said.

Mrs Coop stared at the display cabinet.

'No,' she said, 'I'm not going.'

Mrs Bamber lifted Mrs Coop's hand and pressed the cane into her palm:

'What do you mean you're not going?' she said, and as the taxi hooted, she closed Mrs Coop's hand.

Mrs Coop gripped the cane, then she opened her hand:

'I'm not going,' she said, and she watched the cane teeter forward.

Grabbing the cane, Mrs Bamber raised her voice:

'Of course, you're going: Malcolm's waiting for you,' she said.

'Well, he can wait,' said Mrs Coop. 'It makes a change, him waiting on *me*,' she said, and she leaned to the right and prodded the cushion. 'It's slipped down the crack,' she said. Then holding the remote control backwards, she pointed it at the television. 'What's that shouting?' she asked as outside, the taxi hooted again.

Thirteen

Slouching in the armchair next to the hospital bed Mrs Coop prodded her handbag: it's heavy just there on my leg. She flexed her foot, then repositioned the handbag closer to her knees. She flexed her foot again: that's better; I want to keep my circulation.

Yawning, she continued to trace a finger around the rim of her wristwatch: an hour soon goes, though. There's not much you can do in an hour. After hearing the toilet flush, she listened for the hand dryer as she watched the swing doors to the toilets: when Dorothy says an hour, she means an hour from the time we get here, not an hour from the time *she* goes.

As the swing doors opened, Mrs Coop tapped the glass on her watch face: it should be an hour from the time *she* goes. Calculating, Mrs Coop did not look up when the clack of Mrs Bamber's heals stopped at the foot of her bed.

'I'll just be going now,' said Mrs Bamber, and watching the heart monitor, she raised the back of one hand to her nose and inhaled the lemon scent. Then she repeated herself, twice.

When Mrs Coop did not answer, Mrs Bamber raised her voice and said again that she was just leaving. Then after Mrs Bamber said it a fifth time, Mrs Coop answered, without looking away from her watch.

'You'll be back at twenty-five to one?' she said as she continued to follow the second hand on her watch with her finger.

'No, I'll be back by twelve-thirty,' said Mrs Bamber. She twisted her earrings, then started to button her coat.

Clicking her tongue, Mrs Coop glanced sideways at her husband, then inspected her watch:

'That's not an hour. It's twenty-five to one; that's an hour from *now*,' she said.

Mrs Bamber flexed her fingers.

'Twenty *minutes* ago, you didn't want to visit Malcolm at all. It was only me who convinced you.'

Mrs Bamber put on a glove while Mrs Coop squeezed the bottom of her handbag, then consulted her watch again:

'When you picked up my watch, did they ask what happened to Malcolm?' she said.

'Yes, they hope he gets well soon. You already asked me that,' said Mrs Bamber, and looking out the window, she slipped on her other glove.

Then as Mrs Coop tapped her foot on the linoleum, she looked at her husband:

'No, I meant did they ask why my watch was there fore so long,' she said. 'They know Malcolm's tight with his pennies,' she added.

Mrs Bamber raised a glove to her nose, and as she sniffed, she flexed her hand inside the red leather.

'Right, well, I'm off,' she said.

'It was there well over three *weeks*,' said Mrs Coop. 'I'd have gone myself, but I don't like the Market, not these days since it's gone downhill. It's not like it used to be.'

'Right, well, I'm just going,' said Mrs Bamber. 'I'll be back for twelve-thirty.'

As she stepped away, Mrs Coop reminded her:

'The curtain needs pulling round,' she said. 'I can't visit if it's not private.'

Mrs Bamber shifted her handbag from one should to the other. Then she undid the top button of her coat, and as she reached for the curtain, she lost her balance and bumped against the next bed.

'Sorry,' she said, and she waited, but the man in the bed didn't stir.

'Dorothy, I can't see you,' said Mrs Coop as she watched the curtain being drawn around her. When the curtain stopped near the wall, Mrs Bamber's head poked through the gap, and Mrs Coop hiccupped. 'Oh, there you are!' she said.

'Now I've got to be going. I'll be back in an hour,' said Mrs Bamber.

Mrs Coop inspected her watch: she means an hour from the time we get here, not an hour form the time *she* goes. It should be an hour from the time she goes. That would make it twenty-five to one.

After consulting her watch, Mrs Coop addressed the gap between the wall and the curtain:

'I'll see you at twenty-five to one,' she said. Then leaning forward in the armchair, she peered at the aisle beneath the edge of the curtain: well, I don't see Dorothy's shoes. She leaned back in the chair. 'Fancy having red for best shoes,' she said, and she cupped a hand around her ear: I don't hear them either. 'Dorothy?' she said. '*Dorothy?*' She looked at her watch, then felt for the handbag in her lap: well, she must have gone then. She might have said good-bye.

Slouching in the chair, Mrs Coop regarded her husband: they should shave him. They should shave him twice a day the way he likes. He wouldn't want everyone seeing his nose like that. When Aunt Aggie noticed, she offered to make him something up.

'What hairs?' he said, and he claimed he never noticed them before.

After lifting the sag of her stomach, Mrs Coop leaned forward: I don't see that vein on his forehead. She craned her neck: he's calmed down anyway. I'll give him that: he loses his temper, and then he's pleasant as punch. He can't help it, though: he always blinks twice when he's lying.

I'll never forget that Tuesday I went down on my own to see for myself: well, it was like they said: his car was parked outside the Willacy caravan. The windows were steamed all up, like they said.

'Malcolm,' she whispered, 'what have you done with my savings stamps? They're not yours, you know.'

She bit her lower lip: when he came back for his tea, he could tell I'd seen his car parked there plain as day.

His tea wasn't ready like he thought it would be.

'You've got the monk on,' he said. 'What's up?'

I looked at him: I looked him straight between the legs; then I fed Fee: I gave her a lamb chop, and she scuttled right off with it.

'You're not giving her *that*!' he said.

When he'd gone out, I fed Fee until she was full: she ate nearly all his lamb chops, and when he came back home, he woke me up to apologise.

Then he asked me did I know Fee had been sick on the sofa.

Mrs Coop waited: he's pleasant as punch, and then he puts a flower in that jar on the kitchen window. I tell him I deserve dozens.

'Don't get carried away,' he says.

As she clasped her handbag, Mrs Coop's good eye narrowed:

'You're the thief, not me,' she said. 'I should tell the police what you've done with my savings stamps; they're *not* transferable.'

She waited.

'They'd throw the book at you,' she said, and she rubbed her forehead, then lowered her voice. 'Going with a girl her age: that's disgusting!' she concluded and she looked at her watch.

'Is that the time?' she said. She rubbed the watch face, then looked again at the minute hand. 'Malcolm,' she said, 'just tell me where you've hidden them, and I won't mention another word about that Willacy girl.'

Counting backwards with her eyes closed, Mrs Coop waited; then she opened her eyes.

'I've brought you Marmite,' she said, and she looked at the drips on the other side of the bed; then she watched the heart monitor; he'd prefer a television.

Mrs Coop undid the clasp on her handbag, and as she regarded her husband, she felt inside for the jar.

'It's cold inside,' she said.

She frowned; then with both hands, she stretched the handbag open, and squinting, she looked inside: what I could do with is my toilet torch. She shivered: it's the air from outside that's made it so cold. Her good eye widened; then she hesitated: that looks brown. Feeling in her handbag, Mrs Coop closed her fingers, then withdrew her hand and held the bottle up to the window.

'No, it's just those tablets for my eye patch; they're not tantalisers,' she said.

She set the bottle in her lap, and tapping her feet on the linoleum, she watched her husband's forehead: he's always in a good mood after he's eaten. I'll stand a chance then. She looked down at the linoleum: there's me tapping my feet again! She tucked her feet beneath the chair, then peered insider her handbag and inhaled deeply: it smells of Marmite. It must be here somewhere.

With one hand, she started to rummage: I don't see it. She removed a clump of tissues, and holding them to her face, she flared her nostrils: it's definitely Marmite. She dropped the tissues onto her lap, then wiped the end of her nose: it's sticky. She tasted the tips of her fingers: it's Marmite.

Spreading her legs, Mrs Coop turned the handbag over and emptied its contents onto her lap: there's the teaspoon; it must be here somewhere. She set the empty handbag on the bedside cabinet, then sifted through the objects in her lap: well, there isn't much, just my cassettes and my other things.

Feeling cold steel, she ran a finger across the teeth of her husband's comb: it's *his* things mostly that I carry since that nurse asked me to look after them. With both hands, she picked up a clump of keys: what *does* he do with them all? There must be two *dozen*! She counted, then stopped: there might be one to that caravan with the Willacy girl!

Mrs Coop's face went rigid as she scrutinised her husband.

Then after several moments, she dropped the keys on top of the cassette tape, and staring at her husband, she wiped her good eye: he's definitely getting smaller. She regarded the rack of drips on the other side of the bed:

'Malcolm, you've got to eat something proper, or they'll be nothing left! You'll slip through a *grate*,' she said, and she inspected the length of her husband: he's as think as a rake, these days.

As she regarded the pile of objects in her lap, she felt inside the sleeve of her dress; then with the corner of her husband's handkerchief, she dabbed at the patch on her eye: I don't know where it's got to, that Marmite. She sniffed: it smells like him: it smells like smoke and earth. She closed her good eye: I can just about picture it. I had that Marmite last when I forgot my cane, and when I slipped, they put me in that wheelchair before Dorothy pinched my hand. She pinched it in the spokes before she wheeled it away: I wasn't ready.

Squinting, Mrs Coop rubbed the tips of her fingers over her husband's keys: no: now I'm getting confused. There were roses here beside his bed when I didn't have my cane, but Malcolm prefers freesias. Peering at her husband, she twisted her wedding ring: no: Dorothy said his *cheeks* were rosy; that was it. I can picture him, and his cheeks weren't anything like rosy: they were *grey*. It's been twenty years since his hair was black.

More than twenty: it's not been black since before the Willacy girl.

Mrs Coop opened her good eye: he looks peaceful. She pinched the end of her fingers: of course, he always puts on a brave face when he's not eating: it was only the once when he had trouble with his bowel.

'I'm sorry, Malcolm,' she said. 'If I'd have known something like this would happen, I'd have redeemed them *with* you.'

As Mrs Coop stared at her husband, she wiped her good eye.

'It's all water under the bridge,' she said.

She dried the tips of her fingers on his wallet.

'This fold is wearing through,' she said as she stroked the crack in the leather wallet,' but he won't hear of buying a new one these days, not since they closed that barber's shop. He sold them on the side. He also sold umbrellas,' Malcolm said.

Mrs Coop drummed her fingers on the wallet; then her head turned abruptly as she looked towards the end of the bed:

'Maybe I put the Marmite in my coat,' she said. 'I might have put it there with Dorothy always carrying my handbag. She wants me to pay for her taxi.'

Mrs Coop gripped each arm of the chair as she started to stand: then hearing the clatter at her feet, she cringed: that's not Dorothy's shoes; *they're* red! She bit her lower lip: I've not dropped it, have I? Malcolm prefers glass jars, but Dorothy could have bought plastic: Malcolm won't see the difference.

She lowered herself back into the chair, then leaned forward and looked down past her knees: no, I can't see. She pressed her feet against the linoleum and rolled the chair back from the bed. Then she scanned the floor, and concentrating, she scratched her head: it's just that bottle of pills. It's the rattling inside that confused me with clacking.

Eyeing the bedside cabinet, Mrs Coop rolled the chair forward; she glanced at her lap, and as she felt the top of the cabinet for her handbag, she sniffed: the flowers still smell nice. Malcolm would like that; he can't see they're not freesias.

She set her handbag on her knees, then stared at the roses: of course, they're starting to go over; they're *shrivelling*! She looked at her lap, then picked up her husband's comb and returned it to her handbag; then she continued removing items until her lap was empty: no, it's definitely not here. She looked towards the end of the bed: my coat's the best bet.

She set her handbag on the bedside cabinet, then pushed it back until it touched the wall by the window: the last time I left it on the ledge, Dorothy knocked it over when she pushed by to look at the view. I told her buildings don't make nice views:

'They're too cluttered,' said Mrs Coop.

She shifted her weight forward as she gripped both arms on the chair: when Dorothy turned around, that's when she knocked over my handbag, and I'm sure she saw them: she was talking about the new football grounds one moment; then next thing she's asking me if I'm all right for the toilet.

Mrs Coop shook her head.

'As if it's any of her business,' she said, and she started to stand, then paused: where's my cane? I've not forgotten it again?

She inspected the end of the bed; then she eyed the railing in front of her, and listening, she scanned the length of her husband several times before she reached out:

'There it is. I thought it was part of his bed!' she said, and she stretched for her cane. 'Dorothy's always putting it too far away!' she said, and she rolled the armchair forward, then reached again, and when she grabbed the cane, she twisted. 'It's stuck; it's hooked up on that top railing,' she said.

As Mrs Coop pulled the cane, her chair rolled forward until her knees touched the side of the bed. Then with one hand on the bed railing and the other hand on the arm of the chair, she lifted herself, and as the chair rolled backwards slightly, she stood, then rested with both hands gripping the railing on the side of the bed.

She flared her nostrils as she looked through the window: they're too many these days. She watched the pigeons on the ledge, then glared at the radiator: it's Malcolm's heat they're getting. Narrowing her good eye, Mrs Coop observed the pigeons: Aunt Aggie always called them rats with wings. She tilted her head to the side: I don't know, though: Popsy certainly liked them.

She looked down at her husband:

'I'm just getting your Marmite,' she said as she watched his lips, then inspected his forehead.

She waited.

Then leaning on her cane, she took several steps sideways until she stood swaying at the end of the bed: of course, if Malcolm hadn't lost his temper….She hung the cane on the bed railing, and listening, she felt for her coat: I bet I've put it I here with Dorothy always wanting to carry my handbag. I prefer talking the bus, but she always has me pay for the taxi. Listening, Mrs Coop examined first one pocket and then the other: no, just my scarf and gloves and some tissues. She searched the pockets again: and a bus ticket. She crumpled the ticket and slipped it in the gap between the foot of the bed and the mattress, and after she removed the cane from the railing, she examined her husband: he's defnitely getting smaller. His face is *swamped* in that pillow!

She listened: it's that tube in his nose that makes his breathing raspy.

Leaning on her cane, Mrs Coop moved around the side of the bed. Then blinking twice, she stared down at her husband's abdomen, and after hooking the cane over the top railing, she reached through the bars and touched him lightly with one hand.

She waited, then her good eye widened, and teetering, she took a step backwards: I felt it then: a *kicking*!

I feel sick.

Mrs Coop rubbed her hand and looked at the rack of drips on the other side of the bed: maybe he is getting something proper down him?

She stared at his abdomen, then felt her own: of course, that toast on the floor in the back room was gone this morning, and Dorothy never said a word. Maybe he did eat them afterall? I told him he could if her tried:

'Make your good better,' she said, and she gripped the bed rail with both hands and stepped sideways until she stood at the top of his head.

Then she watched his oxygen tube: of course, that'll interfere with his taste. It'll be like having a cold. Listening to the drill on the road below, she looked out the window: he could do with some tar off those road works.

She looked at her watch, then at the armchair: I'll give my ankle a rest; it's aching. After she lowered herself into the chair, she scrutinised the gap between the wall and the curtain, then parted her legs slightly.

'Where have you been, mucking your plot?' she asked.

She wiped her forehead: I did warn him. I told him to mind his blood pressure:

'That vein's rising in your forehead,' I said.

Mrs Coop opened her mouth and stuck out her tongue: well, I'd almost forgotten about those savings stamps. She listened as she watched her husband's heart monitor: don't think about it.

'Home,' she said. She said it slower. 'Home,' she said.

Her good eye twitched: I only asked him to move the cabinet because I wanted to hoover: there were pine needles in the carpet from that tree of his, and when he got back I was still cleaning.

He didn't offer: he just watched me sort Polly's Indians, and it wasn't until I got to Aunt Aggie's silver tea set that he started on about having thieves in his own home.

Mrs Coop listened: don't think about it. Think it out peaceful like that doctor says on the tape.

'*Home*,' she said.

'*Your* home?' I said. 'Since when is this *your* home?'

She took three deep breaths.

So he starts on about all his so-called modernising, and that's when it happened: I'd never seen his face go rigid like that before.

Then he…then he….

Mrs Coop took a deep breath: think about something else.

She wiped her forehead: maybe it's the change again. It happened twice to Aunt Aggie, but she was always repeating herself.

'Home!' said Mrs Coop, '*home*,' she whispered.

She studied her husband: he looks peaceful enough now. She leaned forward and whispered:

'Malcolm, I'll share them if you tell me where they are.'

She waited.

'We could go on *holiday*. We could go on holiday to that island you're always going on about with the 'c' in it, the Scilly Island.'

Gripping the armchair, Mrs Coop stood, then approached the bed.

'We could go where they have those special trees at their Tescos.'

Gripping the rail, she jiggled the bed:

'We wouldn't have to fly.'

She pursed her lips.

'Malcolm, if you're not speaking, you can at least bat an eye.'

She waited, listening.

'I didn't mean to; it wasn't my fault. It was the Willacy girl that caused it. I was all for leaving after I saw you and her in that position.'

She listened: Polly was always on about me visiting.

'There's wide open spaces; you can walk for miles without seeing another living soul,' she said.

But I never did get there.

Mrs Coop listened to the church bells: I opened the privy door, and when I saw him kneeling, at first I thought he was being sick, and then I saw her, and then I saw where his *face* was.

Mrs Coop reached for her cane:

'It was a goose on one side, and a gander on the other,' she said, and leaning on her cane, she stepped sideways to the end of the bed. Then she hung her cane on the bed rail while she put on her coat, and after she paused through the gap in the curtain, she turned to retrieve her handbag.

'See,' she said, 'I'm not always leaving things!'

When she reached the reception desk, Mrs Coop nodded at the two nurses; then her good eye widened:

'There you are. I was just coming to get you,' said Mrs Bamber, and she twisted an earring as she inspected Mrs Coop.

Fourteen

After the bus pulled away, Mrs Coop thanked the young man in the Mohawk for helping her down the steps with her trolley, and she told him again about her boss's hair on a Saturday in the Market Hall before they changed it.

'They really used to queue at *ours*,' she said, and she stared at the young man's hair as he spat on the pavement. 'It was black like a real red Indian's,' she added.

Then her good eye widened as the young man stepped out onto the Knightsbridge Road:

'Car!' she said, and when the Reliant Robin hooted, Mrs Coop gripped her cane tighter as she watched the young man in the Mohawk thump a fist on the car's bonnet, then weave his way through the traffic to the other side of the road.

As he hoisted himself over the wrought iron face, Mrs Coop grinned: it's smart that fence with its gilded shuttlecocks on top for spikes. Looking up, she scanned the building's façade until she spotted the white clock face: it makes a lovely gong, that, not a bit like that old whistle used to screech at India Mill's.

Shading her good eye, she inspected the clock: of course, the D'Radcliffe's clock's better when the sun shines: it's full of gold. She listened to the screech of buses breaking, then headed for the zebra crossing, and as she waited, she eyed the fence: not gilded, but *painted* gold, those shuttlecocks are. Otherwise, folks would steal them. She grinned as she looked up at the clock face, then nodded as two women stepped around her to cross the road.

'It was nice of Billy to tell me when we were here. It's ages since I've been.'

She shook her head: not Billy Mampy. It's just his hair that reminded me. I didn't ask his name.

Leaning on her cane, Mrs Coop let go of her shopping trolley. She stroked the front of her zebra skin coat as she watched the taxis queue on the other side of the street: of course, taking the bus, I would have preferred getting off further down the Knightsbridge Road.

Looking to her right, her good eye widened as she noticed the bin next to the lamp post: I nearly forgot that. She turned back towards her shopping trolley; then as she started to bend down, her face went rigid: well, I can't put his meals in here. What would people think? Standing, she rubbed her bottom, then turned away from the trolley.

'I'll go to *Woolworth's* after; there's plenty of bins there,' she said, and she tipped her shopping trolley onto its wheels and plodded forward with her cane: it's smooth, this crossing. She stopped to inspect the stripes: we'd never seen a zebra until Aunt Aggie brought her fur coat home from the widower's. Aunt Aggie said the widower kept its head on a wall in his study.

'They look just like stripey horses,' she said, 'only with glass eyes.'

Then she told her story about the woman in Starr Mill with the glass eye.

Wheeling her trolley, Mrs Coop watched the stripes beneath

her feet: they're not like that bumpy ride I had on the elephant; I never wanted to go on another one after that. She frowned: it had hair on its back as well.

As her shopping trolley was jolted, she bumped into the person next to her, then stopped.

'Well, *they* were smooth,' she said.

She waited until the man squeezed past; then she stepped forward with her cane, and when she reached the other side of the road, she pulled her trolley over the bumps in the paving slabs edging the kerb. 'If I was blind, these would trip me up,' she said, and she nodded at the street sweeper: it's nice to see they still keep everything tidy.

Avoiding the crack in the pavement, Mrs Coop stepped forward with her cane: of course, at one time they arrested you for dropping bus tickets outside D'Radcliffe's. She inspected the pavement: there was that coloured woman they fined for dropping her bus ticket. The manager said they didn't often get customers of her type at D'Radcliffe's.

Watching her best shoes, Mrs Coop stepped onto the glazed tiles: I always like these. They make a nice pattern, like an oriental carpet. She bobbed her head at the tiles:

'Like an oriental carpet,' she said, and with the toe of her best shoe, she polished the pattern: it's a shame to step on them.

Pursing her lips, she looked at the sky, then grinned at the flags: it's them fluttering; *that's* the sound: it's *waving*.

She ducked as a pigeon swooped. Then after testing the spot on the tile with the nub of her cane, she stepped sideways and looked up again:

'There's no awning,' she said as her shopping trolley jigged sideways.

Steadying herself, Mrs Coop frowned as the teenage girls linked arms again; then she regarded the banner above the revolving doors: maybe they've sent their awning away to be cleaned? She read the banner:

'Well, it's not so grand without that awning,' she said.

Swaying, Mrs Coop watched the doors: I'd rather have them send those spinning doors away: they're like that teacup waltzer at Blackpool. I thought I'd never get out.

Examining the crowd, she scanned the entrance: there's no top hats; there's no white gloves. She stepped forward, then waited in front of the nearest door: I'll just wait for the doorman. She tilted her trolley off its wheels, then rubbed her elbow after the gentleman bumped into her.

'I'm sorry,' he said, and he ushered her into the revolving door.

As she pressed against the glass, Mrs Coop shut her eyes, and when she felt the rush of hot air, she stumbled forward onto the marbled tiles.

'Steady on!' said the gentleman behind her, and he moved Mrs Coop's trolley to the side of the entrance.

Mrs Coop nodded, then stepped towards the fountain. At its edge she stopped and positioned her cane to avoid the flattened cigarette pack; then inhaling, she looked up:

'Now that's just as grand! It sprays every bit as high as that one at the special exhibition,' she said, and she teetered backwards as she watched the top of the fountain.

Sniffing, she reached inside the trolley for her handbag: I can smell that gammon. I can smell that mint sauce and all those yakums. She scanned the area, then undid the clasp on her hand bag before a lady in a red sash interrupted.

Mrs Coop blushed, then sniffing, she took the red and white striped leaflet.

'Thank you,' she said, and she put it inside her handbag.

With her mouth agape, Mrs Coop watched the young lady as she adjusted her sash, then moved off to speak to the mother and child sitting on the edge of the fountain: she must be posh to work here. She sounded posh the way she said it with her *h's*.

Mrs Coop tilted her trolley onto its wheels, then followed the young lady.

'I have savings stamps,' she said. 'Is it still down the stairs to redeem them?'

The young lady pointed at the escalator.

'Yeah, there,' she said, and she stepped away.

Mrs Coop eyed the escalator: well, it didn't used to be. It used to be down the double winding staircase. Going down them, I felt like in those films with Fred Astaire. *Swingtime*! Those were the days.

Craning her neck, Mrs Coop looked for the stairs: well, you *used* to go downstairs to buy them, I remember. She watched the young lady's red sash: maybe she said it was *down* there? Frowning, Mrs Coop followed: she might have said *down* when she pointed. When the young lady finished speaking to the businessman, Mrs Coop inquired:

'Is it *down* to redeem them?' she asked.

'Yeah, down past the balloons,' said the young lady, and she pointed to the escalator,

'Thank you,' said Mrs Coop, and she turned away: I told Malcolm; they'll have records. It's like Aunt Aggie losing her bonds. When she wrote, they sent new ones: they even sent a pound she'd

won; it was unclaimed, they said. As Mrs Coop neared the
escalator, she stopped suddenly in front of the fountain to examine
the water for pennies.

'That's silver!' she said; then wincing, she teetered on the edge
of the marble wall.

'I told you to stop kicking! Now look what you've done!' said
the mother. 'I'm sorry. We didn't see you,' she said, and she set her
child on the floor, then stooped to pick up Mrs Coop's shopping
trolley, and as the child started to cry, the mother lifted the flap and
put Mrs Coop's handbag and the two knotted carrier bags back
inside the trolley. 'Shut up!' she said to the child. Then she softened
her voice as she addressed Mrs Coop. 'Are you all right?' she said,
and she picked up the child, then continued past the fountain and
out the revolving door.

When the mother had gone, Mrs Coop let her cane dangle
from its hand strap as she rubbed her hip; then she touched her
forehead: I'm flushing. She felt for the strap around her wrist, then
gripped her cane, and hesitating, she looked at her shopping trolley:
never mind dropping a bus ticket. Here's me coming into
D'Radcliffe's with carrier bags from *Woolworths*!

'Are you all right?' asked another lady with a red sash. 'You're
better off taking the lift,' she said, and she wheeled Mrs Coop's
shopping trolley to the lift between the escalators. Then while she
waited for Mrs Coop, she handed out leaflets to the other
customers.

'It used to be downstairs,' said Mrs Coop. 'It used to be down
the double winding staircase. The stairs were *marble*,' she said as she
stood next to the young lady in the sash.

'You're right,' said the young lady, and when the lift arrived,
she put an arm around Mrs Coop as she waited for the shoppers
getting on and off. 'Can you just make some space?' she requested,
and the two businessmen stood back, making room as she helped
Mrs Coop into the lift.

'Thank you,' said Mrs Coop, and her ears reddened as the glass doors closed. 'Thank you, *madame*,' she said, and suppressing wind, she covered her mouth and shut her eyes as the lift dropped down: it's like that fair ride with your stomach in your mouth.

When the lift stopped, Mrs Coop opened her eyes.

'Is *this* the floor you wanted?' repeated the woman, and she continued pressing the button.

Mrs Coop frowned: we used to say their *cleaners* dressed like royalty at D'Radcliffe's. She stroked the front of her coat as she regarded the woman's denim trousers.

'I have savings stamps; I'm going to Canada,' she said, and she stepped off the lift, then reached back for her shopping trolley.

'Here,' said the woman, and she wheeled the trolley forward. 'I'll give you a lift with that,' she said.

'No,' said Mrs Coop, 'I'm getting *off* the lift now.'

Mrs Coop's stomach rumbled as she stared at the floor: there's no carpet. There's no carpet with the coat of arms on it. Prodding the floor with her cane, Mrs Coop frowned: it's lino!

She looked at her watch; then noticing the staircase, she swung round: there it is: it's the double staircase!

'It's got bunting!' she said.

Then she frowned as the glass lift rose up through the centre: there used to be a statue there in the centre. It was of Queen Victoria on her throne. It was very grand.

She listened: it's noisier than I remember. Sniffing, she gripped her trolley, then headed towards the back: well, I must get to *Woolworth's*; Malcolm's meals are ponging. As she watched her feet, she veered to the left; then she noticed the balloon stand.

'That's nice,' she said, and as she stepped towards the stand, she watched two children walk by with ice creams.

She stopped.

'What?' she said, and she struggled to free her cane from the chair leg. Then she surveyed the area: there's too many chairs and tables. They're *entwining*. She regarded her ankle: I could do with a rest. She inspected her watch again: no, there isn't time. I have to be back for Malcolm's meal.

She sniffed: it's oniony.

Tightening the grip on her cane, Mrs Coop moved past the balloon stand to join the queue, and when she reached the end of it, she tilted the trolley back off its wheels. She adjusted her hat, then examined the Afghan coat in front of her.

'It's like those patterns Polly always used to send me for stitching,' she said, and when the woman glanced over her shoulder, Mrs Coop covered her mouth and her cheeks reddened: that first time she sent me the bald eagle. Only the colours were marked wrong, so I started stitching its head *green*.

'What did you think it was, some bloody parrot?' Malcolm said.

Mrs Coop blushed as she bobbed her head at the pattern.

'Well, I didn't know, did I?' she said.

When the woman glanced over her shoulder, Mrs Coop fingered the brim of her hat; then she looked at her best shoes: it's cramping walking in these. She pulled back her coat sleeve, and after inspecting her watch, she regarded the queue: it's nothing like those we used to get on Saturdays.

When she noticed the gap in front of her, she fumbled for her trolley, then stepped forward: there I go again; at least Malcolm's not here to see me doddering. She stepped forward to reduce the gap between her and the woman in the Afghan coat. I'm forever daydreaming in a queue. She took two steps forward: he was furious that time we went to *Boots* for my prescription. When he finished looking at his magazines up front, he came back to see what was taking me so long, and I hadn't moved an inch.

'What are you doing? Watching paint dry?' he said.

Mrs Coop advanced her cane, then stepped up behind it: well, I couldn't tell him, could I, that I was looking at all those French letters?

Pulling her trolley, she stepped forward again, and when she was near enough, she let go, then watched the sunset on the back of the woman's coat. When she stepped forward again, Mrs Coop lost her balance, and the man behind steadied her by the elbow, then returned her trolley, and as he spoke, Mrs Coop watched the scar on his chin: he's standing too close; there's coffee on his breath. She eyed his hand on her coat sleeve: it's hairier than the zebra!

'Thank you,' she said, and she stepped quickly to catch up with the woman in front of her. 'There's all types,' she whispered, and as she approached the woman, she concentrated on the pattern: there's orange and yellow. She grinned: it might be a rainbow!

When she caught the woman's heal with the nub of her cane, Mrs Coop apologised, and the woman nodded, then stepped suddenly forward: it's several times I've done that.

She waited: it's nice that orange and yellow. It might be a sunrise.

She moved her lips.

'Next,' repeated the girl behind the counter. She eyed Mrs Coop. 'Next,' she repeated.

'I'm next,' answered Mrs Coop.

After she gripped her cane and her trolley, her face started to quiver as she stepped toward the till.

She counted, then opened her mouth to speak.

She counted, then tried again.

'Mrs Coop, seventeen Knott Street,' she said. 'Please check your records.'

Peering through her good eye, she watched the girl's lips move, and as Mrs Coop's face went scarlet, she concentrated: she looked to her left and then to her right, and then she adjusted her hat: don't *hiccup* now! Holding her breath, she listened to the girl in the uniform. Then she answered:

'No, I don't have vouchers; I have savings *stamps*,' she said, and as she stooped, her hat tumbled onto the floor.

While the girl in the uniform waited, she glanced at the man in the queue behind Mrs Coop; then raising an eyebrow, she watched a balloon skim across the ceiling towards the air vent.

'There,' said Mrs Coop. She dropped her pension book and the red and white leaflet onto the counter. 'It's in there who I am; you can check you records.'

As her face twitched, she pressed against her cheek with the back of her hand, then lowered her voice:

'There's wide open spaces,' she explained. Then she gripped her hat as the man with the scar prodded her again.

'So you don't want two super-savers tacos?' said the girl in the uniform.

'No, I want my trip to Canada,' said Mrs Coop.

The girl in the uniform frowned as she took the voucher, then excused herself.

After putting on her hat, Mrs Coop regarded her shopping trolley, then stooped to open the flap.

When she stood up, she scowled at the manager; then she tapped her pension book as she looked at the girl in the red and white striped uniform.

'What's the problem,' repeated the manager.

'I want my stamps. I want to redeem them,' said Mrs Coop.

She repeated herself, then tapped her pension book.

The manager inspected her papers, then gave Mrs Coop directions to the post office.

It wasn't far to walk, but she could take a taxi, he said, and he offered to call one for her if she'd just wait over there by the tables.

Fifteen

When the bus stopped in the cul-de-sac at the top of the hill, Mrs Coop peered under the seat in front of her, and with the toe of her best shoe, she prodded the end of her cane: no, it's not budging. Listening, she scanned the seats around her: no, there's only me who's left. As she prodded the end of her cane once more, the driver interrupted. He said again that they had arrived at the top of Long Hill, and nodding, Mrs Coop explained:

'My cane's lodged,' she said. She raised her voice. 'It's caught on something. I don't know what.' Tapping her foot, she listened to the driver; then with both hands, she gripped the crook of her cane and twisted, and when the cane didn't move, she stopped and listened again. Then she pulled upwards. 'I can't *lift* it; it's wedged beneath the seat,' she said, and with her free hand, she jiggled the seat in front of her. Then listening, she watched the driver raise the barrier, and after placing a cigarette behind his ear, he stepped down to stand in the aisle.

He said it again as he approached. Then he took Mrs Coop by the arm, and as she rose from her seat, she blushed: oh, he said he'd give *me* a lift. Standing, she opened her mouth, then shut it: no, I won't bother explaining.

With one hand, the driver freed her cane; then he shouldered Mrs Coop's handbag and guided her down the aisle, and when they reached the steps at the front of the bus, he adjusted the cigarette behind his ear, then gripped a lever.

'You're all right, luv,' he said.

As she felt his grip tighten on her arm, Mrs Coop teetered backwards.

'I'm falling!' she said.

'You're all right, luv,' he repeated, and he steadied Mrs Coop.

She batted her eye; then after she had regained her balance, she flared her nostrils as a blast of cold air billowed the bottom of her coat: maybe I should just stay. There's a thousand places he could have hidden my savings stamps; it'll be like finding a needle in a haystack.

She looked down the steps, then sideways at the driver: he smells like Malcolm. She leaned backwards with her free hand, then fumbled over the front of her coat until she gripped the tassel on the belt around her waist. Inhaling, she blinked: when Malcolm started with that perfume, I knew. As the driver guided her, Mrs Coop flared her nostrils, then held her breath as she settled down on the next step: I knew it was that Willacy girl's idea. As her good eye started to water, she sneezed, then looked at the windscreen: I should watch that; I'll get a dew drop. With the fur on the edge of her coat sleeve, she pressed against her nose: I'll get a dew drop or *worse*.

'You're all right, luv,' said the driver, and he pressed against her elbow until she grabbed the railing. Then leaning backwards, she gripped harder as the driver reassured her.

'Only one more?' she said, and tilting her head from side to side, she considered her position. 'Well, it looks like *two* to me,' she added, and she closed her eyes as she was jilted to the ground.

'It's all red!' she said. She stared at the letter box next to the bus shelter and rubbed her jaw: it's unsettling, that landing. I could have bitten my tongue.

'Are you all right, luv?' asked the driver.

Mrs Coop nodded: that last step's winded me.

She waited; then as she took her cane from the driver, she asked for the time of the next bus.

'There's one every hour,' he said, and prodding her elbow, he nudged Mrs Coop with the handbag until she gripped her cane's leather strap.

'There used to be nothing here. I barely recognised the place,' she said, and she looked down the hill as the driver lit his cigarette.

'You're all right,' he said, and after he pointed her in the direction of the allotments, he turned to board the bus.

'I barely recognised it,' said Mrs Coop, and she watched as the bus circled the cul-de-sac. Then as it descended the hill. She put her handbag on her shoulder and covered the end of her nose. 'Give me a tram any day; trams never stank like that,' she said.

She set her handbag on top of the letterbox: do they paint them red for red letter days? Turning her cane sideways. She felt inside the opening, then hung the crook of her cane from it.

'It's sheltering,' she said, and she turned away to regard the town at the bottom of the hill: of course, Dorothy would like the view. There's *miles* of buildings; I barely recognised the place. She stroked the front of her coat: it was only the turrets on Crompton Hall that twigged me after I got off. I thought I'd taken the wrong bus.

She rested her ankle: it seems like yesterday we took a tram to the bottom, then walked up to Crompton Hall. It was the end of the line. She took a deep breath: Aunt Aggie hated the walk, but they always put on a good do at the end of it. She grinned: there were fireworks! Mrs Coop blinked as she left the cold air on her eye: I'll never forget the first time Aunt Aggie saw the girl with the false arm marching in the Whitsunday Parade:

'Look at the glove on her hand,' she said. 'That's *lace*!' Then at Crompton Hall, she told everyone afterwards. 'They needn't have done that,' she said, 'but it was very nice of them for the parade, don't you think?'

Mrs Coop watched the sky: of course, we didn't walk with any church; we went on our own. She looked down the hill: there were no buses up here in those days. In those days you had to walk, and when we got to the top, Aunt Aggie would always say it:

'Well, for once I'm *glad* to be over the hill.'

She examined her ankle: of course, back then I didn't get what she was on about. She frowned at the scuff on her shoe: there's me galloping up Long Hill like there's no tomorrow. She flexed her toes: well, I'd only just learned. It was after that Western we saw, and I wanted to be one of those spotted horses that rode for the Indians:

'An *Apaloosa*,' she said. 'Now there's a mouth full.'

When Popsy told me, Aunt Aggie didn't think I'd remember.

She smiled faintly at her best shoes: I can still hear Aunt Aggie plain as day:

'Slow down, lass; I'm worn out just looking at you!'

She stroked the tassel on the belt of her coat: of course, I'd have been making sparks with my galloping as well, only Aunt Aggie would never let me wear clogs. Whenever I asked, she say that so long as she lived, I'd never work in a mill and I'd never wear clogs, and not even Popsy could convince her.

'Oh, go on,' he'd say. 'What's the harm in clogs for our Elsie?'

But Aunt Aggie put her foot down at that.

Mrs Coop held her chin up: of course, I was full of myself in those days. Whenever we did that walk up Long Hill I said it:

'Why do they call this Long Hill?'

Then Aunt Aggie would give me a clout around the ears with her fan.

Mrs Coop twisted the heal of her shoes into the earth, then rubbed her good eye: well, Aunt Aggie never stood for any cheek.

She squinted: after all those years we walked up Long Hill, and I hardly recognised the bottom of it! There's me getting off the bus....What was that dye works called? She looked down the hill: when I was little, there was that sign at the bottom: it was a white skull and cross bones.

'I thought there were pirates!' she said.

She shook her head: well, it wasn't anything to do with pirates; it was a warning to mind the low overhead pipes: it was the end of the line.

She frowned: that housing estate blocks the turrets on Crompton Hall. They're always building new houses. She turned away from the town, and stepping to the side of the letterbox, she steadied herself in the wind, then looked over the moor towards the sea: there used to be nothing this end: just wide open spaces. Polly liked that.

She grinned: them were the days.

Teetering, she put a hand on the letterbox, then braced herself against the wind: Malcolm always says you can smell the sea from his allotment. She sniffed: well, you *can't*. She sniffed again: you can't smell anything *like* the sea.

She blinked, then rubbed the tear from her good eye: it's the wind that does that; it's stinging!

After Aunt Aggie died, I thought it many times: it's us now's the old ones, Malcolm. There's no one else left.

She cupped her hand over her eyebrow and regarded the horizon: it's all changed these days. It's not like it used to be. She turned her head towards the right: it's over there somewhere. You can see it on a clear day. Sniffing, she scanned the horizon: it doesn't feel like something you can see from home; when you go there, it seems like a different country…of course, I've never been to a different country, but that's what it seems. Turning her head, Mrs Coop followed the clouds further to the right: he thinks I'm daft, but I know what I mean about Blackpool Tower feeling like a different country. You could be in Paris.

She frowned at the Lake District: after I broke my ankle, I told him I wasn't going to any countryside again. She looked further towards her right: some forest he took me to: there were hardly any *trees*. Malcolm was always so stingy like that. I told Aunt Aggie after:

'We have more trees in Grand Venture Park,' I said.

Mrs Coop shook her head at the clouds.

'Those clouds look like sheep sleeping,' she said. Then her good eye widened. 'Except for that black one; it's not sleeping; it's going to rain!'

She put her handbag on her shoulder, then took up her cane, and watching her shoes, she stepped forward: it makes me lopsided walking like this. She stopped to wipe her index finger across her nose; then she scanned the field above the allotments: that Willacy girl wasn't crafty at all getting Malcolm to wear that perfume. As the wind gusted, Mrs Coop put both hands on her cane to steady herself: of course, Malcolm was forever shaving, but he only put it on when he was going to see that bicycle.

Feeling the weight of her handbag, Mrs Coop squeezed her shoulder: I knew. She lifted one hand off her cane, then feeling for the cowl, she pulled it up over her head: I knew and I could *still* smell her perfume on top of it all.

'If she'd have been crafty, she'd have stopped wearing *that*,' she said, and flaring her nostrils, she sneezed as she inhaled grit from the cul-de-sac.

Then after wiping her good eye, Mrs Coop shrugged her shoulder: it feels like that driver's pulled my arm out of socket. She rubbed against the fur stripe: I'll bruise; I bruise like a peach!

Sneezing, she touched the patch on her eye, then after steadying herself against the wind, she cupped her hand over her forehead as she peered at the field above the allotments: if that caravan's still there, I'll pull his plug. She watched the field: that time we were in the centre of town, and the Willacy girl calls out from across Market Hall Street. She shouts, so everyone could hear it:

'Good morning, Mr Freckle!' she says, and she giggles. 'How's Mr Freckle? Did he rise and shine early this morning?' she says.

Then Malcolm's ears went bright red.

Well, he only has one freckle. It's more like a mole, actually.

Mrs Coop concentrated on placing her cane: well, that caravan wasn't here when he brought me to see those special flowers he'd grown. She scanned the edges of the cul-de-sac: I'd have preferred a new *Prestige* pressure cooker.

When she came to the lay by, Mrs Coop frowned: he parked just there in the mud. She glanced toward the sea, then looked back at the letter box: when I asked him who the letterbox was for, he said they couldn't build houses up here because of the viewing point.

She walked past the triangulation marker: they were going to, but they stopped it. She watched her feet, then stood still at the top of the path: the Ramblers stopped it, he said. She looked down at the allotments: last time I nearly fell over, and after Malcolm caught me, I told him I had a bad feeling. I asked him why he couldn't bring his flowers up to the car, but he insisted. He was very proud about it: he wanted me to see them in their various *stages*.

She prodded several cobbles on the path with her cane: I was right too with my bad feeling. Testing, Mrs Coop positioned her cane in the middle of a cobble, then stepped down the path, and as her handbag started to slip from her shoulder, she paused and adjusted the strap. She stepped forward again, then hesitated: there's a cobble missing.

'Gone are the days when I played hopscotch on cobbles with Mary Clegg and the rest of them,' she said, and she placed her cane in the space, then turned to look back up the path: no, I can't see that letterbox, not even the top of it.

'There's grit,' she said, and as the cowl billowed, she gripped the edge and pressed it against her forehead, then continued down the path.

'Home,' she said.

She repeated it with each step, and when she reached the first allotment, she stopped to yawn, then looked up at the sky: I like sheep; I always have done. She looked at the slug on the cobbles: I never counted them jumping over fences, though. I couldn't picture it: well, they're too high for sheep to jump.

As she moved forward, the flesh on her arm jiggled, and she tried again:

'Better,' she said as she pressed her cane into the slug.

Then after several more steps, she stopped. She let go of the cowl and wiped the end of her cane on the edge of a cobble before she looked down the row of allotments: fancy gardening on a hill!

Dig for Victory? Dig for backaches more like.

She waited.

Of course, he was pleased at first when his allotment was at the end of the row:

'That way I can expand it bit by bit,' he said, and he did until they added that one on next to it.

He always thought it was Dorothy who told them about his fencing.

Tightening her grip on the cane, Mrs Coop walked forward: of course, Malcolm always says the Cromptons only donated the back of Long Hill to bribe the Council for that statue of Lady Muck outside the Market.

'Where there's muck there's brass,' Malcolm says, and he raps her statue before he opens the door for me.

Mrs Coop stopped.

'I always tell him: it's bronze, not brass,' she said.

Of course, her real name wasn't Lady Muck.

She turned and looked back up the hill: that time we had that flood, and everything he planted washed away over night.

'It's a river gushing down the whole back of Long Hill!' he said.

When he told us, I kept thinking: no more brussel sprouts. No more gooseberries. No more gi-normous turnips.

'What if that happened when the War was on? We'd have starved then,' he said.

Well, Aunt Aggie put him right:

'You didn't have your allotment then,' she said, and she

reminded Malcolm how it was Polly who was always bringing us bits and pieces.

Mrs Coop listened: no, it's too early for birds singing. She pursed her lips: of course, Malcolm was furious about that flood. He was so cross he talked in his sleep, so I had him sleep downstairs. She yawned: not in the front room; Aunt Aggie wouldn't have that.

'If he talks in his sleep, then he can try sleeping in your Popsy's old chair in the kitchen,' she said.

Mrs Coop listened, then stopped to look over the fence.

'*Chickens!*' she said. 'Now why couldn't he keep chickens?'

She pulled the cowl off her head: all those years of powdered eggs; then all he's interested in is growing special turnips. *Hybrids*, he calls them. She wiped her nose: when he started off on his hybrids *this* and his hybrids *that*, Aunt Aggie said that nothing tasted any better.

'Your brussel sprouts *still* taste like passed wind,' she said.

Mrs Coop stepped forward: of course, she said the same about boiled eggs, and she was always onto him about how he should keep chickens instead.

Well, I stuck up for him: it was because of their lice that Malcolm wouldn't keep chickens. It was after the dance he first told me: he said you'd spend two hours plucking, and you'd be covered in lice. When he told me that, he started at the tips of my fingers, and he creeped his hand up my arm until he reached my neck.

'There were hundreds of them,' he said, 'and that's how it felt as they crawled up, then got trapped under your collar.'

After that, he ducked me into the doorway of that barber's shop next to the Co-op and kissed me.

'So I quit that job and took up gardening,' he said, and he kissed me again.

Nearing the end of the allotments, Mrs Coop slowed her pace: I told Aunt Aggie it was like her with spiders, but she insisted chickens are nothing *like* spiders. Then she told us how in her day it was only on Easter Sunday that they ever got an egg of their own.

'The rest of the times we only got the top of our parent's eggs,' she said.

Then Malcolm would have a go at her:

'Easter? I thought your family never went to church,' he'd say.

When Mrs Coop reached her husband's allotment, she looked back up the hill: it looks a mess with everything all mismatched and higgledy-piggledy. She watched a bin liner blow across the path: of course, it's warmer at the bottom out of the wind. Malcolm's always going on about that:

'Mine's more sheltered than the rest,' he says.

Shifting her gaze, she stared at the padlock on the gate; then she removed her handbag and hung it from the gatepost. She waited until her handbag finished swinging; then she undid the clasp and felt inside for his keys.

'I'll just have to work my way through them one by one,' she said. She tried the first two keys. Then on the third key the padlock sprang open when she twisted: he's right; he *does* keep everything well-oiled. He's always saying so:

'If I didn't keep on top of things, everything would go to pot, I'm telling you,' he says.

After opening her coat pocket, she dropped his set of keys inside, then set the padlock on top of the gatepost before she opened the gate.

'Here's the boggy bit I've fixed up,' he says.

Hesitating, she tested the gravel on the path with the tip of her cane: it seems all right. It's not so loose. Pressing down, Mrs Coop stepped forward, and as she passed the clump of snowdrops, she kept her eye focused on the path: of course, my savings stamps could be anywhere. She listened as her cane crunched pocks into the gravel: they might not even be here at all.

When she reached the greenhouse, she stopped, and after shifting her weight, she lifted the end of her cane and tapped against the glass: he could have hidden them in here, even. She tapped harder, then lowered her cane: no, someone might see them.

She looked at the end of the path: his shed's more likely. She glanced inside the greenhouse, then stared at the bar and padlock across the door: when he brought me here, I told him I couldn't see the point of that: if someone wanted to, they could just break the glass. She rubbed the patch on her eye: if they saw that padlock, they might think they *should* break the glass.

Mrs Coop continued down the path: when I saw my special flowers, I asked him:

'Are those hybrids from the silly island as well?'

He knew what I really wanted was a new *Prestige* pressure cooker.

Standing below the scarecrow, she stopped to inspect the raised beds: he wouldn't hide them under there, would he? With the tip of her cane, she prodded the carpet: that time he tried to hide that mark he made on the carpet next to his armchair. He thought he could move the lamp to cover it, but first thing I did was trip when I came in to dust: *honestly*!

She lifted the edge of the carpet: no, he wouldn't hide them out here in the weather. She looked up at the sky: it's not starting to spit, is it? Of course, I've no umbrella. She held out her hand; then as it began to hail, she hurried towards the shed at the bottom of the path.

When she reached it, she stopped at the ramp leading to the doorway: no, it wasn't at the top; it's just here, the old boggy bit. Everytime I come, he shows me how many feet it was boggy after the flood. I've only been so many times, and *each* time he shows me. Then he explains about raising the shed.

She looked up the ramp:

'It's not for wheelchairs; it's for my wheel*barrow*,' he said.

As her cheeks started to quiver, Mrs Coop took a step backwards and waited: he's always going on about them. She watched it sitting still by the bottom of the shed door. He says it's the chickens that draw them. After several moments, she shook her head: it's not a rat! It's the boot scraper hedgehog I bought him!

Mrs Coop felt her way up the ramp and when she reached the door, she propped her cane against the doorstop, then retrieved her husband's keys from her pocket: of course, he won't mark them, not even with an initial or a dab of paint.

'Well, I might *lose* them,' he says.

She dropped a glove: he never loses anything. She examined the keys: that's the house. That odd one's for his car. She paused at the next key, then tried the one after it: no, not that one. Mrs Coop tried the next key, and after the lock opened, she dropped the padlock into her pocket, then pushed open the door, and glancing at the doorstop, she picked up her cane and entered the shed.

Once inside, she sneezed: it's that damp that does it; it's musty. It must be bad for you, breathing it in. She wiped her forehead, then glanced at the window to her right before closing the door.

After that, she wiped her nose, then felt inside her pocket: if my stamps are here, they could be anywhere…like finding a needle. Wheezing, she clutched the penlight, and after she observed the size of the spot it made in the wall, she blinked: I hope I didn't leave it on since whenever. She clicked off the beam, then clicked it on again, and she shined it in the corner, away from the deck chair.

'More rakes!' she said. She lowered the penlight: well, honestly: I don't know what he does with them all. 'He'll be wanting a hoover next with all of those carpets,' she added.

She moved the penlight back to the left. Then cringing at the sound of hailstones pelting on the roof, she shined the light up and down the wall.

'That isn't ours; we *never* had deck chairs,' she said, and she inched sideways. Then stopped when she felt an obstacle against her leg. As she pointed the beam at it, her good eye widened: more coils of hose? No wonder he needs a wheelbarrow carting all that around.

'The things I do, woman. The things I do to put food on the table.'

He sounds like a broken record saying that.

Besides, it's me who puts food on the table. It's me who clears it away as well!

She shook her head at the object: no, not a hose: it's my puff!

With the toe of her shoe, she nudged it, then frowned: when I asked what happened to that, he said he'd thrown that. She nudged the puff again: I bet it's mouldy underneath. She put her foot down: no: I can't shift it.

She looked out the widow: it's deafening, those hailstones. She raised an eyebrow, then pointed her penlight at the wicker armchair next to the window: it looks like a *throne* with that high back on it.

She listened as the hail pelted against the roof, then she looked down at the armchair: well, he does treat himself, doesn't he! The next time he goes on about my thermal tights, I'll remind him about the throne he keeps at his allotment. She nudged the puff with the toe of her shoe: he told me he'd thrown that.

She held her hand up to her mouth and exhaled. Then with her lips pursed tightly together, she waved the smell away.

'It's that Marmite; it doesn't mix with butter,' she said, and she felt inside her coat pocket, then removed a roll of indigestion tablets before she fumbled with the wrapper: it's cold; it's *stiffening* cold in this shed.

She tried again: I can't do it with one hand, not in this cold. She swallowed, then set the penlight on the table next to the oil lamp, and after undoing the top two buttons of her coat, she reached inside, then put on her glasses: they're minty, my tablets. She held one up to the light in the window, then shrugging her shoulders, she placed the tablet on her tongue, and as she chewed, she returned the roll of tablets to her pocket.

Then she turned to examine the wall of shelves: my stamps could be anywhere. She lifted her sleeve, and shining the penlight, she looked at her watch, then pressed against her bladder: the bus driver said it's every hour, and they come and go at the same time, so it's not like Dorothy. Mrs Coop's stomach rumbled: they'll deliver his meal to her if I'm not in. She'll keep it warm. Meals on wheels, Dorothy calls them. Well, they're not on wheels; they're on tin trays.

Mrs Coop stepped towards the shelving; then she stopped, and opening her mouth, she continued to wheeze: it's this must. Malcolm's always wheezing when he comes home form his allotment. She turned, and with the penlight, she inspected the wicker armchair: it's a bit low. Wheezing, she shined the beam from the floor to the seat of the armchair, then estimated: it's lower than our chair by the telephone. She flexed her ankle: it's cracking; I better have a look at those shelves first.

When she reached the shelves, she stopped and scanned the wall with the penlight: this whole *wall's* shelves. It's *shelves* from floor to ceiling. She puffed out her cheeks: I recognise those: they're from Aunt Aggie's bedroom. They're like mahogany. She scanned the shelves again: it'll take more than an hour; it's like finding a needle in a haystack. Of course, they're always in bales. They're always in *rolls* these days, not stacks.

She pursed her lips, then touched the patch on her eye before she stepped closer to the shelves, and blinking, she tried to read through the glint on the labels: those look like insecticides: *sprays*! He's always going on about them. As her good eye watered, Mrs Coop reached to pick up a bottle, but when she felt the glass, she withdrew her hand. She waited, then fumbled inside her coat pocket: nothing here; just his keys. She felt inside the other pocket: no, I've forgotten my gloves. After rubbing her hand against her coat, she stepped forward, then sniffed: yes, definitely.

She sneezed.

'Bless you,' she said; then she sneezed again, and she covered the end of her nose; then she took a step backwards and looked up at the top shelf: of course, if it's up there, I've no chance. She looked over her shoulder at the wicker armchair: well, I'm not standing on *that*. I'd go straight through the bottom. Her stomach growled as she scanned the shelves with the penlight, and when she saw the rat poison, she waited: imagine feeding them that. When Dorothy went on about it being good for strokes, I told her what they used to give P.O.W.s in their rations.

She bit her lower lip: so what have I done with it then? She looked out the window: I might have left it. I'm *always* leaving things. Dorothy says that about my handbag. She's always warning me. Mrs Coop twisted the tassel on her coat: well, maybe it's here? Pursing her lips, she strained to keep her good eye from twitching: it might be in here. Sometimes I can't see for looking.

She aimed the penlight at the door, then at the puff.

'Home!' she said as the light zigzagged over the deckchair.

'Home!' she said as her face contorted.

She breathed deeply, then swallowed as she steadied the bean on the wicker armchair: no, it's not here. It's *definitely* not here.

She listened: well, I better go and see.

She listened: at least the hail's stopped; it never lasts for long.

After negotiating around the puff, Mrs Coop opened the door, then stepped onto the doormat, and listening, she wiped her feet, then continued down the ramp, and when she reached the bottom, she paused to twist the tip of her cane into the hail covering the gravel. She listened: it's rumbling. It's not thunder. She looked at the sky, then pressed her stomach: it's not me.

She waited, then started up the path, and when she reached the greenhouse, she stopped and leaned on her cane with both hands: I'm flushed; I can feel it. She felt her forehead, then looked at the path behind her.

'It's hard going in that gravel,' she said. 'It's too deep. It's *deeper* with hailstones.' Then raising a hand to her face, she looked at the path ahead of her. 'Turnips!' she said as the tip of her thumb poked into her good eye.

She waited; then after she wiped her eye, she looked down the path: it's the gate. I've left the gate open! She shook her head: I'm always leaving things! I hope it's still there.

She checked her best shoes; then after she reached the gate, she stopped and looked up at the sky: it's *rumbling*. Listening, she cupped a hand around her ear:

'No, it's *gushing*, that sound,' she said, and she shook her head at the stone well on the other side of the path. 'Malcolm won't like that so close, not after his flood,' she said.

She inspected her watch: the driver said the next one was in an hour: now what time did he say that?

She considered the sky: I'll be waiting in the dark at this rate. At least I've not forgotten my toilet torch. Her good eye watered: that aeroplane's flying low. I can see it flashing. She ducked: it's reversing? It'll crash if it's not careful.

Covering her ears, she looked at the well across the path: it's not safe waiting in the dark. It was broad *daylight* when they did it to that poor old dear from Blackburn: three of them did it to her.

'Home,' she said.

It was broad daylight, in her own home as well.

Mrs Coop watched the sky, then looked at the open gate: they *knew* her! Well, one of them did. She kept getting her husband's paper after he died. He collected the money; he was only a lad.

The old dear didn't want to stop getting her husband's paper.

'Home,' she said.

Mrs Coop buttoned her coat, then stepped through the gate, and after she spotted her handbag on the gate post, she cowered.

'I've forgotten my trolley!' she said, and when she heard her name repeated, she looked up at the sky, and her good eye widened as she heard it repeated again: there's no shelter. They're no sandbags.

'Polly!' she said.

She turned and stepped back inside the gate, and after she closed it, she covered her ears and looked down at her best shoes:

he'll tell me I had it coming; I'm always leaving things, he says. It's like that chain on the front door: I should know better; I should know best!

Sixteen

Mrs Coop felt for her eye patch: no, it's gone now; I keep forgetting. She looked at her watch: the bin men will have come this morning. I told Dorothy this isn't my home. There's no pagodas, and there's radiators in the bedroom. Malcolm doesn't like it hot in the bedroom.

She wiped her forehead.

Malcolm would like the view, though. I keep telling him.

She folded her husband's handkerchief, then slipped it under the cuff of her cardigan: it's hot enough to bake bread in here. Dorothy says so when she visits.

'It's the change,' she says. 'I can't stay for long.'

Then I tell her:

'No, it's these radiators. They're not even under the window!'

Mrs Coop touched her eyelid: I keep forgetting.

She drummed her fingers on both arms of the chair as she sat beside the bed: well, of course, I knew how to Lindy. I wouldn't have been there if I didn't know how to Lindy! She looked at her watch; then reaching out with one finger, she pressed the red light on the wall. At first she pressed gently, but then she pressed firmly with some time, without relief: of course, there were mirrors at the séance; the dwarf was too small for anyone to see at the back of the room. No: the *spirit* was too small. She waited as her face jawed in time with the tapping of her foot: I knew how to waltz as well. We knew all the dances, Polly and I.

When she heard the voice over the intercom, Mrs Coop's face went rigid, and her pupils dilated.

'This room's got a pong,' she said, and she pressed harder on the light.

When the nurse arrived, Mrs Coop lifted her finger, then folded both hands in her lap: she's like that canary whistling. She's shrilling like a teapot. She waited until the nurse fell silent. Then she looked up and made her request.

'Malcolm needs some buttered toast and Marmite,' she said, 'and he'd like some gammon for Bob Bash. It's to *wake* him….'

She paused, and while the nurse interrupted, Mrs Coop stared down at the freckles on her fingers: she'll fly away one day, like a canary whistling like that.

No: she'll keel over.

'Fee!' she said.

When the nurse finished declining the request for special food, Mrs Coop continued.

'Bob Bash told us he'd been dancing with Polly. She's still very tall, he said,' and raising her voice, Mrs Coop extended her request. 'Polly would like a siamese twin goose: a *real* one, not two geese stitched together,' she added.

The nurse declined once more; she scratched her hip, rubbed it against the doorframe, then asked if there was anything else.

'Malcolm would like some buttered toast and Marmite, *please*,' said Mrs Coop.

The nurse rubbed her hip against the doorframe again, then suggested the bar of chocolate on the bedside table, and when she offered to open it, Mrs Coop informed her:

'Dorothy bought *me* that,' she said, 'but *Malcolm* always likes buttered toast and Marmite before he goes to bed. He prefers it *burned*,' she added, and feeling pulses throb in her eyes, she watched the nurse's trainers crossing the wet linoleum.

'They'll steal those. They'll steal those right off your *feet*,' said Mrs Coop, and she opened her hand as the nurse snapped off a piece of chocolate, then pressed it into Mrs Coop's palm.

As Mrs Coop opened her mouth, the nurse explained once more about the meaning of the red light. When she'd made herself clear, she set the remaining chocolate on the bedside table, and as she squeaked across the floor, Mrs Coop said so again:

'That's what they did to that poor old dear from Blackburn,' she said.

The nurse examined herself in the mirror on the back of the door. She swallowed the chocolate, then warned Mrs Coop again about the red light. After that, she opened the door and stepped back outside.

'You'll end up like Peter and the Wolf,' she said, and she shut the door.

Mrs Coop waited: there weren't any *wolves* when I turned on the light; he was just like that *monkey* with it, watching the Willacy girl.

Unblinking, Mrs Coop rocked in the armchair as she sucked on the chocolate: it's melting; it's lovely when it's melting: it's like *butter*!

She stopped rocking.

'It's better than *butter*,' she said, and she swallowed, then lifted herself out of the chair. 'That's better,' she said, and she stood stiffly on the wet linoleum. 'Home,' she said, and as she regarded the dresser across the room, she counted down. 'Nine, seven, nine, five, *one*!' she said, and she took off suddenly.

When she reached the dresser, she toppled the collection of plastic red Indian dolls; then she took a step backwards.

'I've ruined his rows,' she said.

Wheezing deeply in her throat, she focused on the object in the middle of the silver tray: Malcolm wouldn't like that.

She removed the urn; then with both hands, she lifted the tray, and turning, she paused to stare at the wet linoleum: after I pressed the light, I told the nurse it wasn't me who was sick on the floor; it was Aunt Aggie with her indigestion. I told the nurse Aunt Aggie doesn't like brussel sprouts. If I've told her once, I've told her a thousand times.

'They're *hybrids*!' she said.

Counting, Mrs Coop stepped forward until she reached the chair. Then she sat and polished the tray in her lap with a tissue. When she finished, she dropped the tissue onto the floor next to the bin, and as she leaned forward, he breasts sagged onto the tray: it's too far away.

She sat back in the chair, and with two fingers, she tweaked the wings of her nostrils; then she leaned forward and clawed the lace runner towards her.

'It's heavy; it's fattening,' she said, and when the bar of chocolate overhung the edge, she gripped it. 'You won't slip through,' she said. 'There's no grates.'

Then biting her lower lip, she set the chocolate and the wrapper onto the tray, and she stared at the bedside table: there's that glass of water to soak my teeth. She leaned forward to move the glass off the lace runner and onto the bare part of the table next to the lamp: it won't stain what I've spilled, at least.

'Water's not soiling,' she said, and humming, she plucked tissues from the box, then dabbed at the pool of water on the lace. After that, Mrs Coop held her breath while she straightened the lace: it's wrinkling.

She tossed the tissues at the bin, then sat back in the chair and closed her eyes.

'Home,' she said, and after several moments, her breathing slowed, and her head drooped forwards, bobbing slightly until she raised it. 'Home,' she said, and she reached out and began to break the bar of chocolate into segments: it's soldiers.

'Malcolm,' she said, 'there's buttered toast and Marmite.'

Counting, she arranged the pieces end to end along the edge of the tray, and when she finished, she turned over the wrapper of gold foil and smoothed it onto the tray. Then with the nail of her index finger, she wrote into the foil.

'*M* for Malcolm,' she said, and she rearranged the chocolate, placing it on the foil in the shape of the letter: everyone likes chocolate. It's better than spirit water.

When she finished, Mrs Coop smiled faintly at the letter; then she frowned: it's four. She removed a piece of chocolate: it's lopsided. She sniffed, then rotated the tray until the letter faced the red light. After that, she stared at the red light, and moving her lips, she counted backwards:

'One,' she said, and she stuck out her tongue, then withdrew it, scraping chocolate onto her gums: I've forgotten Malcolm again. I'm forever leaving things.

After rubbing her eyes, she lifted the tray and set it on her bedside table. Then she stood, and pressing the ball of her left foot against the linoleum, she tested the surface. She nodded, then tested with her right foot before she crossed the floor to the dresser.

When she reached it, she nodded at the plastic flower in the jar, then picked up her husband's urn, and holding it against her chest, she returned to the armchair: I promised Malcolm he wasn't going to that garden, not after what those winds did to Aunt Aggie.

She set the urn on the tray next to the chocolate.

'There's no television,' she said, and she picked up the tray, then lowered herself into the armchair, and when she sat with the tray in the centre of her lap, she rotated the urn and stared as the red light: it's better than a candelabra: there's no wax *dribbling*!

She clapped her hands.

'Home,' she said, and whispering, she rubbed her eyes, then began counting, and when she finished, she glanced at the red light, then rotated the urn: it's like a miniature pressure cooker. It goes well with Aunt Aggie's silver tea set. It's better than those special flowers.

'Thank you, Malcolm,' she said, and as she looked down at the top of the urn, she sniffed: scented dahlias, he called them. That was it: *dahlias*.

'Dahlias would be a nice name for someone,' I said. 'It's a shame to waste a name like that on flowers.'

Mrs Coop rubbed the top of the urn:

'Malcolm, if you tell me where my savings stamps are, I'll share them. We can go to that silly island,' she said. She raised her voice. 'The *Scilly* Island, I mean.'

She waited; then she slouched back in the armchair and rested her head against the antimacassar as she stared at the red light: I told Polly it's no use clapping. It doesn't go off when you clap. There's no switching it.

'Never shall I rest,' she said, and she flexed her ankle.

Malcolm was right about our honeymoon:

'It wouldn't have happened if you'd listened to me; we should have gone cycling,' he said, 'not *rambling*.'

I was only thinking of the cost of hiring those two cycles. Rambling was free. It was more a weekend away than a proper honeymoon. We could never afford a proper honeymoon.

Mrs Coop looked at her watch, then whispered:

'Home,' she said.

She waited.

He was right about the cycling, but I didn't want to go. I didn't want to go on one of those tandems.

'I'm not going. Imagine the view!' I said, and I put my foot down, so we walked: we went rambling instead. That was the start of it.

Mrs Coop placed the tray on the bedside table, then looked at her watch:

'It's nearly three. That's when they finish,' she said.

She stood, then stepped to the window and waited.

'There's thousands of them, all in short skirts; they're *younger* than that Willacy girl,' she said. Then she turned and looked at the urn on the bedside table. 'Malcolm, if you tell me where my D'Radcliffe's saving stamps are, I'll let you have a look.'

Blinking twice, Mrs Coop stared first at the clouds and then at the horizon.

'There's no place like it,' she said.